This book belongs to

_____

_____

Disney
Big Book of Fun
Girls'
Time for Friends

Pages 10–13 | SURPRISING MAGIC TRICKS
Script by Tea Orsi, layout and clean up by Marino Gentile, inks by
Santa Zangari, color by Studio Kawaii.
Pages 34–39 | SEALED WITH A KISS
Adapted from the story *Sealed with a Kiss*, written by Melissa
Lagonegro, illustrated by Elisa Marrucchi.
Pages 43–48 and 65–70 | PROM NIGHT NIGHTMARE
Manuscript by Valentina Camerini, layout by Stefania Fiorillo, clean up
by Stefania Fiorillo and Stefano De Lellis, inks by Marina Baggio,
paint by Gianluca Barone, graphic illustrations by Gianluca Panniello.
Pages 72–75 | BUTTERCUP THE BRAVE
Adapted from the story *Buttercup the Brave*, written by
Catherine Hapka, illustrated by the Disney Storybook Artists.
Page 98 | ONLINE TUTORIAL
Manuscript by Silvia Lombardi, art by Paolo Campinoti, inks by
Roberta Zanotti, paint by Roberta Zanotti, graphic illustrations
by Gianluca Panniello.
Pages 102–105 | MYSTERY TEARS
Script by Tea Orsi, layout and clean up by Gianluca Barone, inks by
Santa Zangari, color by Studio Kawaii.
Pages 130–135 | TIANA AND HER UNUSUAL GUEST
Adapted from the story *Tiana and her Loyal Friend*, written by Natalie
Amanda Leece, illustrated by Studio IBOIX and Walt Sturrock.
Pages 138–141 | VOLLEYBUG
Script by Marta De Cunto, layout and clean up by Marino Gentile,
inks by Santa Zangari, color by Studio Kawaii.
Page 161 | A FRIEND BY YOUR SIDE
Manuscript by Valentina Camerini, art by Paolo Campinoti, inks by
Roberta Zanotta, paint by Angela Capolupo, graphic illustrations
by Giuseppe Fontana.
Page 164–167 | A SWEET ROYAL VISIT
Adapted from the story *A Royal Friend*, written by Lisa Ann Marsoli,
illustrated by the Disney Storybook Artists.

This edition published by Parragon Books Ltd in 2015 and distributed by

Parragon Inc.
440 Park Avenue South, 13th Floor
New York, NY 10016
www.parragon.com

ISBN 978-1-4748-1170-5

Printed in China

Disney
Big Book Girls' of Fun
Time for Friends

PaRragon

Bath • New York • Cologne • Melbourne • Delhi
Hong Kong • Shenzhen • Singapore • Amsterdam

Healing Power!

NOT JUST EMERGENCIES!

When a fairy or a sparrow man comes to the Urgent Fairy Care, they must first be evaluated for urgency before being admitted to a treatment room.

All patients are examined with great care by the nursing-talent fairies. Whether it's a pinched finger or a fairy caught up in a frog's tongue, every sickness is taken care of with the right remedy!

In the Urgent Fairy care, there are baskets with berries and seeds, healthy food, and magnifying lenses. You certainly won't find . . .

Circle the item that doesn't belong in Urgent Fairy Care:

Berries and seeds

Magnifying lens

Paint sprayer

Healthy food

6

Answer on page 171

In Pixie Hollow, there's a place where the smell of essences and medicinal herbs fills the air. Hurt fairies fly here for healing!

WING PROBLEMS

The first time Tinker Bell wound up at the Urgent Fairy Care she had frozen wings because she'd crossed the border between warm and cold realms without a single precaution!

A healing-talent fairy warmed her up with two lightning bug lamps, then examined her wings with a magnifying lens. Luckily nothing was broken, and she was prescribed just two sunflower seeds!

Quiz: The Music For You

YOU'D LIKE TO BE WOKEN UP BY...

A BIRDSONG

A FESTIVE BAND

YOU LOVE LISTENING TO MUSIC WHILE...

DRAWING IN YOUR DIARY

WITH FRIENDS

THE MOST FLITTERIFIC SOUND IS...

THUNDER CRASHING

A GURGLING WATERFALL

HARP

You and SILVERMIST both adore the sound of water, whether it's gentle rain or the roar of a tumbling waterfall. The music of stringed instruments like the fairy harp reminds you of water and gets your wings moving!

Complete these sentences, follow the arrows, and fly straight to your profile! You'll discover your own talent for music and the instrument that's right for you!

WHEN YOU'VE GOT A SONG IN YOUR HEAD, YOU...

TAP YOUR HAND OR FOOT

HUM OR WHISTLE

DRUMS

For you, music is the pitter-patter of a lively bunny! You move to an upbeat sound and so does FAWN. You'd be great on a percussion instrument like the fairy drums!

SOFT RAINFALL IS...

UNWELCOME

A PRETTY MELODY

FLUTE

Like your pal TINKER BELL, you enjoy working to the snappy beat of birdsong! You'd certainly make wonderful music with a wind instrument like the fairy flute!

Surprising Magic Tricks

IT'S A PERFECT DAY TO RELAX IN THE SUMMER GLADE . . .

IT'S SO PEACEFUL!

I JUST MIGHT TAKE A NAP!

UGG . . . I SPOKE TOO SOON!

MAKE WAY! COMIN' THROUGH!!

MAKE WAY FOR THE **MAGICIAN** OF PIXIE HOLLOW!

?!

WHAT'S INSIDE?

YOU'LL SOON FIND OUT!

I'M HERE TO THRILL YOU WITH MY AMAZING **MAGIC SHOW!**

MAGIC?!?

YOU?!?

OK, EVERYBODY, TAKE YOUR SEATS! THE SHOW IS ABOUT TO BEGIN!

ALRIGHT ALREADY!

LET'S SEE WHAT YOU CAN DO!

AS YOU SEE, MY HANDS ARE EMPTY!

NOTHING UP FRONT, NOTHING BEHIND MY BACK!

YUP!

BUT . . . ABRACADABRA!

VOILA! A CARD FOR YOU, MY LOVELY AUDIENCE!

WOW!

INCREDIBLE!

BUT . . .

CRAAAAAA

AAAHHH!

GULP!

CLANK PUTS THE LID BACK ON IN A FLASH . . .

YIKES!

THAT LOOKED MORE LIKE A **CROW** THAN A RABBIT TO ME!

MAYBE YOU USED THE WRONG MAGIC WORDS . . .

NOT AT ALL! THAT WAS A RABBIT . . . ER . . . **DRESSED** AS A CROW!

CRAAAAAA

I'D SAY YOUR BUNNY IS QUITE THE CONVINCING ACTOR!

SIGH!

HA HA!

THE END

13

Best Time for Sport

When summer comes and the weather is fine, Merida loves practicing archery while riding Angus. What aim she has! Trace the twirling paths of the arrows along the dotted lines.

After such a ride, Angus deserves a tasty treat. Connect the dots to see what it is!

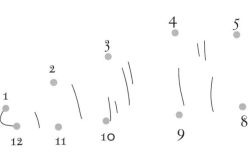

14

Answer on page 171

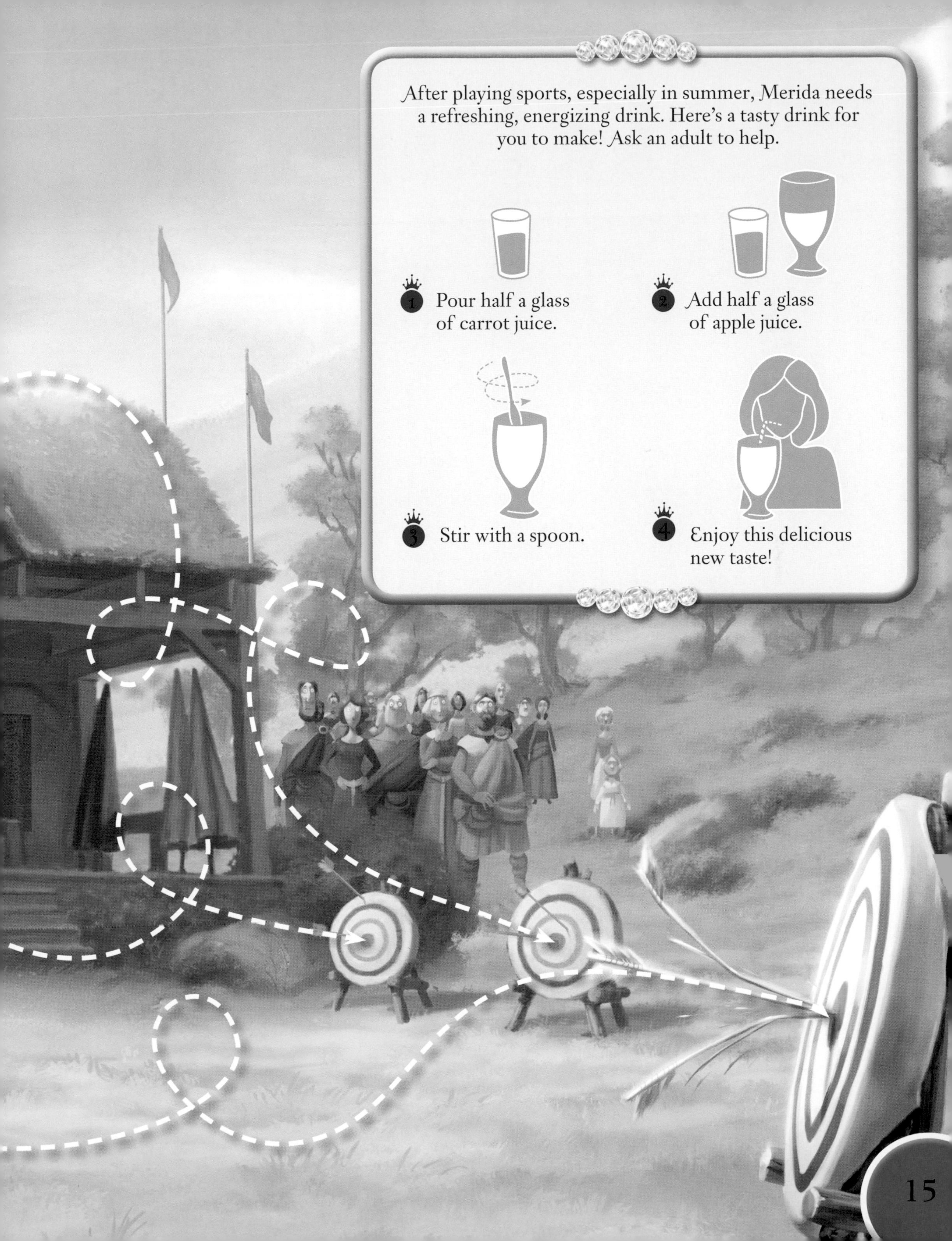

After playing sports, especially in summer, Merida needs a refreshing, energizing drink. Here's a tasty drink for you to make! Ask an adult to help.

1. Pour half a glass of carrot juice.

2. Add half a glass of apple juice.

3. Stir with a spoon.

4. Enjoy this delicious new taste!

Summer Dream

Merida is getting ready to enjoy this afternoon the way she likes best. One of these two scenes shows her plan. Check the correct one.

Follow the lines and write the letters in the spaces provided. What does Merida have in mind?

e

r s o e h i d r n g i

16

Answers on page 171

A Great Day

Rapunzel is getting ready for the celebration that marks the beginning of summer. Color her in.

Designed by You

DO YOU DREAM OF CREATING THE LOOKS EVERYONE WANTS TO WEAR? GET THE SCOOP ON BEING A FASHION DESIGNER!

If you're always playing around in your closet, creating new outfits and customizing your clothes, you might have a **talent for fashion design**!

Fashion designers create **dresses, suits, shoes, and all kinds of clothing and accessories** that people wear every day. **As a designer, you might come up with a new style** of dress and present it in a fashion show. If it's a big hit, stores will start selling it, everyone will want to wear it, and **you'll have just started a new trend**!

3 Ways Get Started

If you want to make your dreams of fashion design come true, you can get ready now!

1. **Start with magazines**. Anytime you can, look at fashion magazines to study various looks to learn the names of certain styles.

2. **Create a portfolio**. Collect pictures of outfits you like for inspiration. Take note if you tend to like certain styles more than others.

3. **Take an art class**. If your school or community center has a drawing class, sign up! It can help you learn to put your designs on paper.

Quick Check!

Is Fashion for You?

TAKE THIS QUIZ TO FIND OUT!

START

For each question, color **2 BUTTONS** for each **YES**, **1 BUTTON** for a **MAYBE** and **0 BUTTONS** for a **NO**.

1. Do friends rely on your skills to put outfits together?
2. Do you love to shop for clothes and shoes?
3. Do you spend hours putting outfits together?
4. Do you regularly read fashion magazines?
5. Do you watch every TV show about fashion design?
6. Do you experiment with wearing unusual styles and colors?
7. Do you like to draw and sketch?
8. Are you able to sew?
9. Do you ever sketch gowns or outfits you'd like to wear?
10. Do you love window shopping to see how new looks are put together?

If you colored most of the buttons on the meter, **you definitely have the passion for fashion!** If you colored fewer than half, maybe **your love of fashion design just hasn't shown up yet!**

END

Nature's Magic!

Have fun with Clank and Bobble as you solve each riddle!

Clank and Bobble are admiring the newly blossomed flowers. Color the two sparrow men!

Butterflies and Buttercups

Buttercup Canyon is filled with fluttering butterflies. How many of these types of butterfly and buttercup can you count? Write the answers on the lines.

A  ___   C ___

B ___   D ___

E ___

A new fairy trick...

... now that's a real kick! Connect the dots from 1 to 38 to see what hops out of Tink's basket.

Play with the Fairies!

summer Dominoes!

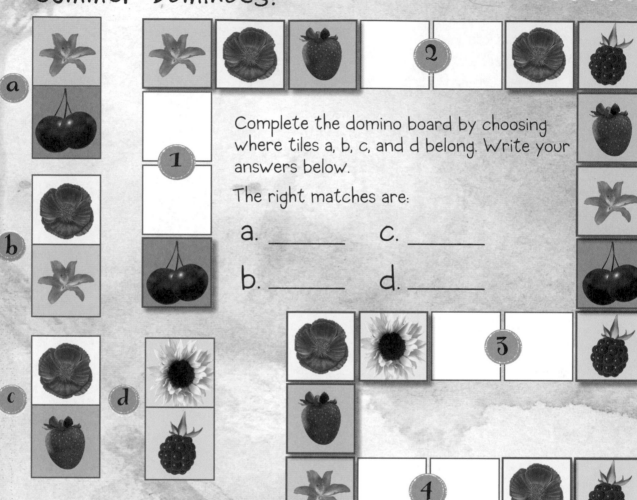

a

b

1

2

c

d

3

Complete the domino board by choosing where tiles a, b, c, and d belong. Write your answers below.

The right matches are:

a. _____   c. _____

b. _____   d. _____

4

Insects in the grid

Draw the ladybug, the bee, and the butterfly in the grid so that they appear only once in each row and column.

22

Answers on page 171

Unleash your talent and help the fairies solve the puzzles!

Tinker Bell's come to cool off in Havendish Stream. Color her in!

Enchanted Night

On the magic night that celebrates the birth of the princess, Rapunzel and Flynn take a boat ride beneath the lanterns floating in the sky. Count the different types and write the numbers in the circles below.

= ○ = ○ = ○

Summer is the season of the sun! Trace the sun symbol and color it in!

A birthday present for the princess! Which of these gift boxes matches the one shown above?

Smell of Roses

When the weather's warm, it's great to spend time outdoors, so today Belle wants to decorate her gazebo with roses in bloom. Help the princess find her way through the maze and pick up the pots as you go!

Answers on page 171

Put the stained glass image of the rose back together!
Write the correct numbers in the right-hand picture.

4 1

3 2

Which flowers has Belle found along her way? Check them off!

Movie Magic

MOVIES CAN MAKE US LAUGH, CRY, OR TAKE US TO PLACES WE'VE NEVER IMAGINED!

Movies can expand our worlds and stretch our imagination, teach us new things, and show us new places. Or they can just make us laugh or weep.

Movie Genres

A type of movie is called a genre. Genres tell you generally what you can expect from a movie: **laughs (comedy)**, **fear (horror)**, **warm feelings (romance)**, or **excitement (action/adventure)**.

Which Genre of Movie is for You?
TAKE THIS QUIZ TO FIND OUT!

Yes

Do you enjoy the dialogue (talking) as much as the action in a movie?

Do you hate feeling tense while watching a movie?

No

Do you prefer movies with beautiful scenery and colors over dark or gritty movies?

POP CORN

Yes

Do you love watching love stories onscreen?

Yes

No

ROMANCE
You love the stories in which couples **live happily ever after**.

Romances tell stories of people and the struggles they overcome to find love.

No

Is it important to have a few laughs in a movie?

Yes

Yes

No

COMEDY
You have a great sense of humor and like movies that make you laugh.

A **comedy** might also be a romance, action, or other type of movie, but it's designed to make people giggle.

ADVENTURE
You like thrills— but not necessarily scares—when you watch a movie.

Action/adventure movies might feature spies, superheroes, or anyone who's doing something exciting.

No

Yes

Do movies ever give you bad dreams?

No

HORROR
You're not scared! Bring on the zombies, vampires, and other spooky stuff!

Horror movies play on our fears and are designed to make our hearts beat faster!

Musical Accompaniment

Triple Shadows

Look carefully at Ariette and Lyra's shadows.
Which one exactly matches the fairy musicians?

1

The correct shadow is: _____

2

3

Answer on page 171

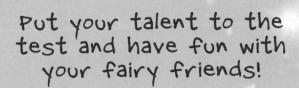

Put your talent to the test and have fun with your fairy friends!

An Eye for Detail

Draw lines to match each close-up detail to the scene where it belongs.

1

2

3

a

b

c

Emergency

Help Lyra get to Urgent Fairy Care by choosing the right path!

A

B

C

Answers on page 171

Flower Trail

Iridessa has gotten lost in the woods!
Follow the trail of flowers in the order
shown on the list to help her find
her way back to her friends.

START

END

purple
blue
pink
orange
purple
blue
yellow
pink
orange
blue
pink
blue
yellow
orange
blue

32

Answer on page 171

Ariette & Lyra

These twins have the same talent but move to different beats!

It's not often that twin fairies are born from the same laugh, like Ariette and Lyra. They look exactly alike, from their golden hair to the tips of their wings. And they're both music-talent fairies!

They dress alike and think the same thoughts! But that's not all! They often find themselves talking in unison! Yet there's something that singles each out. Ariette adores the lively sounds of the flute, while Lyra prefers slower rhythms and bass-driven sounds.

These two lutes are almost . . . twins! Spot the one detail that's different.

a

b

Answer on page 171

33

Sealed with a Kiss

It was a warm summer day, so Ariel and Flounder decided to play hide-and-seek under the sea.

They were having fun, so Ariel suggested asking another friend to join them.

"Who are you thinking of?" asked Flounder.

"What about the baby seal we met a few days ago?" Ariel said, pointing to where the baby seal might be.

Flounder thought that was a great idea, so they went to look for the baby seal.

Ariel swam very fast and Flounder tried to keep up with her.

"Wait for me!" he called.

Finally, they found the baby seal sitting on a rock.

"I'd love to play with you. Thank you for inviting me!" he said.

Ready to play, the three friends swam under the sea together.

"One, two, three . . ." When Ariel started counting, Flounder and the baby seal swam off to hide. Flounder had no doubt about his perfect hiding place, but the baby seal didn't know where to go.

"Ready or not, here I come!" Ariel called. She was sure she'd find Flounder in no time.

"Gotcha!" cried Ariel. "How did you find me so soon?" a surprised Flounder asked her.

She always knew where to find him—he was her best friend after all!

"You'd better change your favorite hiding place next time!" said Ariel.

Then they set out to find the baby seal.

"Maybe he's hiding inside something!" Flounder suggested.

"Good idea!" said Ariel. "I know where he could be! Come with me!"

Ariel pointed to some pirate treasure and looked inside the chest.

Wow! There were so many wonderful things: precious necklaces, jars, and vases. But no baby seal.

"Let's search somewhere else!" Ariel said.

Then she heard some music and thought, "Maybe the baby seal is hiding there, among the musicians and their instruments."

While Ariel searched, Flounder started dancing. But, again, no baby seal!

So Ariel swam back to the rock, but the baby seal wasn't there either. When she saw Scuttle, she told him they were playing hide-and-seek with the baby seal and couldn't find him!

"So you have to call the game just 'hide' and no 'seek'!" Scuttle laughed.

37

Back underwater,
Ariel and Flounder
heard a noise.
"Squeak! Squeak!"
"What is that?"
asked Ariel, worried.
Was it the baby seal
calling for help?

They swam as fast as they could
to reach him.
Oh, no! The baby seal's tail was
stuck in a giant shell!
"Help me, my friends!" he said.

"Don't worry, baby seal,
we'll free you!"
Ariel tried to open the shell.
She lifted, she pulled, she tried
as hard as she could, but it
wouldn't open.

At last, using all her might, Ariel opened the shell and set the baby seal free. How happy they were!

"Thank you, Ariel!" said the seal joyfully.

"You're a really good player, baby seal. But next time we play, you'll be the one who counts!" said Ariel, laughing.

"Yeah, no more hiding," said the baby seal, laughing too.

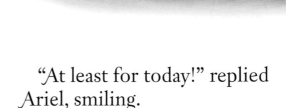

"At least for today!" replied Ariel, smiling.

The game was over, and so was their fun summer afternoon. Ariel gave her friend a big hug and sealed it with a kiss.

"See you soon, baby seal!"

The End

Fun in the Sea

What fun it is to play hide-and-seek on summer afternoons! Help Ariel look for her friends at the bottom of the sea. When you find them, circle each one in the scene and check them off below. Then color them in!

While playing, the baby seal got his tail stuck inside something. Color in the spaces with dots in a dark color to see what it is!

Answers on page 171

41

Playful Pets

MEET LEONARD'S DOG, DANTE, AND MRS. FLAMINGO'S SUGAR GLIDER, SUGARPLUM—THERE'S ALWAYS A LITTLE EXCITEMENT WHEN THEY'RE AROUND!

Sugarplum is a sugar glider, a kind of tiny opossum, who belongs to Daisy's neighbor, **Mrs. Flamingo**. Given a chance, he likes nothing better than to get out of his cage and cause mischief! He's naturally more active at night, and should be sleeping in the daytime. So even though Sugarplum loves sugar, he's not allowed to have it during the day—he goes a little wild!

Leonard's dog, **Dante**, is sort of the group mascot for Minnie, Daisy, Leonard, and Macy. He loves to chase sticks—Leonard has to be very careful with his *Wizards & Fun* wands or Dante will try to crunch them, too! And Dante is always on the hunt for snacks!

MORE ON SUGARPLUM

Personality: Unpredictable, mischievous
Loves: Dark places
Favorite things: Beets and rhubarb candies

MORE ON DANTE

Personality: Fun-loving, curious, chow-happy
Loves: Playing with Leonard and his friends
Favorite things: Food . . . and Leonard, of course!

Prom Night Nightmare!
(Part 1)

DLIN DLON

HERE'S YOUR SHOPPING, MRS. FLAMINGO!

THANK YOU, DEAR! DID YOU REMEMBER THE **RHUBARB CANDIES** FOR SUGARPLUM?

OF COURSE! I BOUGHT HIM A BUNCH!

HOW THOUGHTFUL! **HE** SIMPLY ADORES YOU!

WITH WHAT YOU EARNED THIS MONTH, YOU CAN BUY SOMETHING NICE FOR **TOMORROW'S** DANCE!

OH, I DOUBT I'LL GO. I'LL PROBABLY JUST SPEND THE EVENING WATCHING TV!

HMM . . . IF YOU DON'T HAVE ANY PLANS, I HAVE **SOMETHING** FOR YOU!

43

PANT! PUFF! DAISY SHOULD BE THERE WITH MINNIE!

AND THERE SHE IS!

IT'S GOING TO BE A FANTASTIC NIGHT. I CAN'T WAIT!

GULP!

IT SURE IS! YOU WOULDN'T MISS IT FOR ANYTHING IN THE WORLD!

SHE'S INVITED MINNIE! HOW CAN I TELL HER... THAT I WANTED TO GO WITH HER?!

HORROR NIGHT
HORROR NIGHT

I'M WORKING ON MY GOWN. IT'S GOING TO BE SPECTACULAR!

LATER . . .

SIGH! TOO LATE. DAISY HAS ALREADY INVITED MINNIE!

BUT I'LL ASK HER FOR A TICKET ALL THE SAME! SHE'S A FRIEND. SHE'LL UNDERSTAND!

YES . . . BUT HOW? MINNIE IS HER **BEST FRIEND!** AND HORROR NIGHT IS A ONE-TIME EVENT!

DAISY, THERE'S SOMETHING I REALLY FEEL STRONGLY ABOUT!

THERE'S LEONARD! I'LL ASK HIM TO LEND MINNIE HIS STARS!

DAISY, I'VE GOT SOMETHING REALLY IMPORTANT TO ASK YOU! WOULD YOU LIKE TO COME WITH ME . . .

!

Turn to page 65 to find out how the story ends!

Style Smart

MINNIE MASTERS THE ART OF FINDING ACCESSORIES THAT ENHANCE HER LOOK. THEY ADD THE PERFECT FINAL TOUCH TO AN OUTFIT!

1 A **necklace** can draw the eye upward and highlight the upper torso.

2 A **handbag** shouldn't be an afterthought—it's the cherry on top of the outfit!

3 Use a **bow** for a splash of color or to create a special hairdo.

4 **Bracelets** draw attention to your hands and can add texture to your look.

5 A **belt** can add shape to your silhouette or a bold splash of color.

Your Turn!

Minnie's Bow Pin

Give your outfit a touch of Minnie style with this cute bow pin you can make yourself!

1 Gather two fun fabrics, a colorful button, a pin, and glue.

2 Trace a bow shape on one of the fabrics and a slightly bigger bow on the other.

3 Cut out both bow shapes. Glue the smaller one on top of the larger one.

4 Glue the button in the center of the bow. When it's dry, use the pin to attach it to your outfit!

The fairies and sparrow men of Pixie Hollow are hard at work building a boat. Help them by coloring in the scene!

Animal Pals

Fawn must reach the insects in the meadow. Help her through the maze to get there!

Answer on page 171

Color the crickets hopping playfully around the pond!

Meet Bobble

Lean and merry, he's a tinker-talent sparrow man who loves his work!

His full name is Phineas T. Kettletree, Esquire, but in Pixie Hollow everyone calls him Bobble. He wears large, wood-frame glasses with dew drops for lenses. He couldn't work without them, and a dew dropper that's always handy in case he needs a recharge!

He loves working with Clank and also has a ball as Tinker Bell's assistant. He was thrilled when he got to help her build the snow machine. That's how Periwinkle, Tinker Bell's sister, saw her dream of traveling to warm kingdoms come true!

Bobble is an expert fixer-upper. What about you? Find the piece missing from this container in a wing-beat!

1

2

3

Answer on page 171

Shooting Stars

Jasmine knows that every time you see
a shooting star, you can make a wish.
On this summer night she's made three!
What has she wished for? To find out,
crack the code by filling in the letters
that match each symbol.

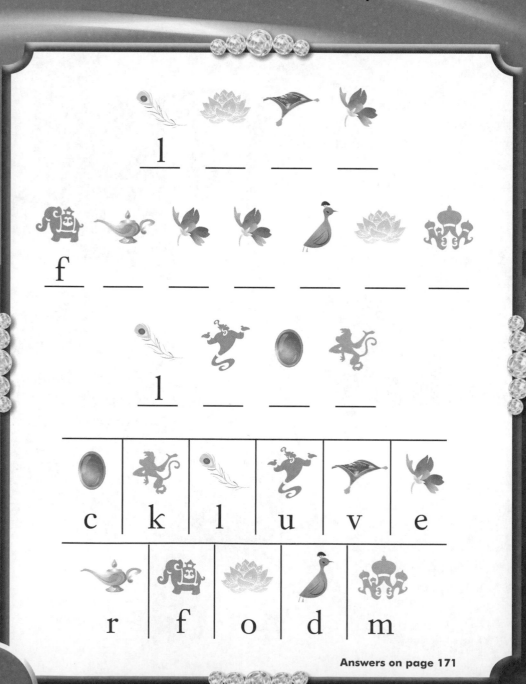

Answers on page 171

Now add some magic to this enchanting summer night. Color in all the stars with gold. The sky will look even more sparkling!

Surprise!

To celebrate the return of their sweethearts, the princesses have made their own romantic balloons. Look at the colors to match up the couples!

WELCOME

The princesses have hung a special banner in the hall for their princes. Trace the letters to see what it says!

Look Sharp!

TICKET TIE-IN
Study the concert tickets below and find the exact match for each.

The right pairs are:
- - - - - -   - - - - - -
- - - - - -   - - - - - -
- - - - - -   - - - - - -
- - - - - -   - - - - - -

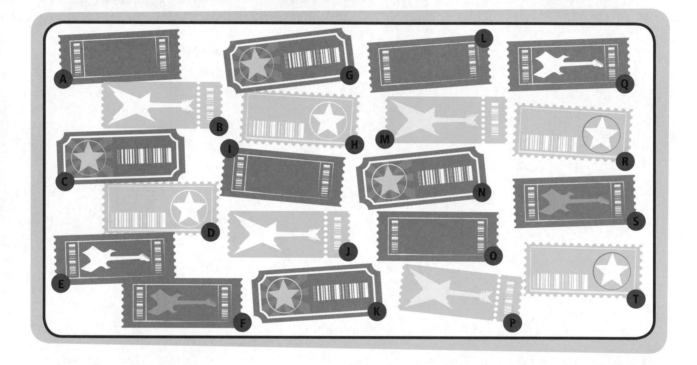

MUSIC MATCH
Which of the earbuds on the right is plugged into the music player? Follow the cords to find out!

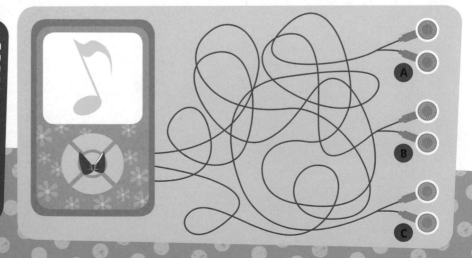

Answers on page 171

Puzzle Play

SALAD SHOPPING

Scan the section on the right and draw a line anytime you find the items below in the exact order listed, in any direction: Pear, apple, melon, potato.

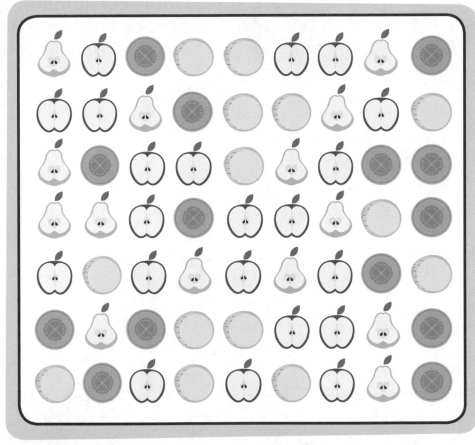

WHICH PET IS WHICH?

Draw a line from the pet to the sentence that describes it.

A Cat

B Dog

C Hamster

D Goldfish

1 I was one of the first animals ever domesticated by humans—more than 10,000 years ago!

2 My tongue is rough like sandpaper so that I can groom away hair and fleas.

3 My teeth are constantly growing, so I need to chew to file them down.

4 I don't have a stomach, so I can only eat a little food at a time.

Happy Music Makers

Playful jumpers and "musicians," crickets bring joy to summertime in Pixie Hollow and on the Mainland!

WHAT MUSIC!

Male crickets have a special talent for music! Like a violinist drawing a bow across the strings of his instrument, these little critters rub their wings together to produce beautiful melodies!

On summer nights, they stand at the entrance to their nests and the concert begins. Their chirping is used to attract females . . . if they like the song that's played!

THERE WHEN YOU NEED 'EM!

In Pixie Hollow, the most musical crickets belong to an orchestra and accompany the music-talent fairies when they perform!

Once Tinker Bell built a cuckoo clock with a cricket inside that chirped every hour, on the hour!

GRAB A CRICKET!

On the Mainland, crickets are often considered a sign of good luck. In China, if a good-hearted person catches one, the cricket makes his or her wish come true!

Do you know the technical name for crickets' chirping? To find out, cross out all the letters that appear 3 times.

CSTYRIBCDU
YBLATBYCION

Answer on page 172

61

Pixie Party!

Once a year, when the moon rises bright and purple over Pixie Hollow, the fairies celebrate with the Purple Moon Party. Join them and have fun!

An Eye for Detail

Tinker Bell, Iridessa, Vidia, Periwinkle, and Fawn have created gorgeous new gowns for the party! Look at the close-up details on the opposite page and match them with the fairies they belong to.

Now play with a friend!

Game Rules:

- Take turns connecting 2 stars with a line.
- When you complete a square, write your initial in it and win 1 point.
- Squares with pompoms are worth 3 points.
- The game ends when no more squares may be drawn.
- The player with the most points wins.

1

2

3

4

5

Star Gazers

Sky Scan

These two illustrations of the night sky might look the same, but they're not! See if you can find the 10 differences in the picture on the right.

Galactic Facts

How much do you know about stars and planets? Answer true or false to the facts on the right.

A **Mars** is the largest planet in our galaxy.
○ True ○ False

B Our galaxy is called the **Milky Way**.
○ True ○ False

C The **moon** is considered a star.
○ True ○ False

D Distances between **stars** and **planets** are measured in light years. ○ True ○ False

64

Story

MIKE?! WHAT ARE YOU DOING HERE?

HAVING A HARD TIME!

WHY'S THAT?

BECAUSE OF THE PROM! I WANT TO GO, BUT I DON'T HAVE THE GUTS TO ASK A *GIRL*!

ANOTHER VICTIM OF THE SCHOOL DANCE! THEY SHOULD ABOLISH IT!

WHAT'S YOUR STORY?

DAISY EXPLAINS WHAT HAPPENED ...

I'VE KNOWN HIM ALL MY LIFE ... BLAH, BLAH ... NOBODY ASKS A FRIEND TO A DANCE IN THAT WAY ... BLAH ... THAT'S WHY I THINK HE MAY BE IN LOVE WITH ME ... BLAH, BLAH ...

INVITE HIM TO THE PROM AND TELL HIM YOU JUST WANT TO GO ON BEING FRIENDS!

GOOD IDEA!

BUT I'LL NEED MONEY TO BUY A *DRESS*!

I CAN BUY THOSE **HORROR NIGHT** TICKETS! THAT WAY I'LL HAVE SOMETHING TO DO TOMORROW.

...AND I'LL RAISE SOME CASH!

DAISY HURRIES TO THE ONLY ONE WHO CAN HELP HER FIND A DRESS FOR THE DANCE **IN A SINGLE AFTERNOON!**

QUICK, MINNIE! I NEED YOUR **HELP!** I ABSOLUTELY HAVE TO GO TO THE PROM WITH LEONARD!

REALLY?! WHAT HAPPENED?

I'LL EXPLAIN IT TO YOU LATER, NOW I NEED A DRESS!

WELL, IT'S YOUR LUCKY DAY...

YOU CAN USE MINE!

THERE'S STILL TIME . . .

" . . . TO FIX THAT!"

MIKE!

YOU CAN GO TO THE PROM! AND WE KNOW WITH WHOM!

?

FANTASTIC! I GUESS I WON'T BE NEEDING THESE!

BUT REMEMBER: DRESS UP FOR THE OCCASION! YOU MIGHT EVEN BE CROWNED PROM KING!

MINNIE, GREAT NEWS! YOU'RE GOING TO WEAR THAT DRESS TONIGHT!

The End

Good Eye!

CANDY COUNT

Study the two jars of candies on the right, then try to answer the questions below.

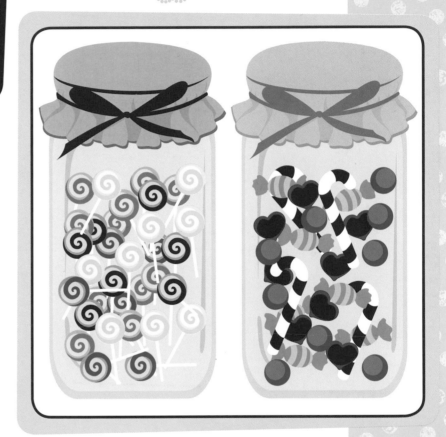

A One of the jars has a **pink lid**, the other is **blue**.
○ True ○ False

B There are fewer **pink lollipops** than **green lollipops**.
○ True ○ False

C The pink jar contains both **lollipops** and **heart candies**.
○ True ○ False

D Both jars have the **same total number of candies**.
○ True ○ False

E The second jar has fewer than **5 candy canes**.
○ True ○ False

Oops!

What a mess! Find the spill that perfectly matches the one next to the bottle.

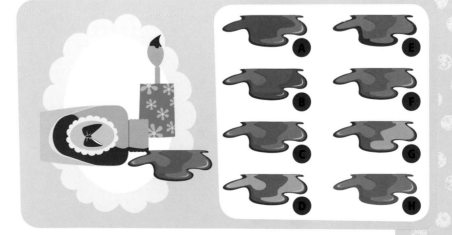

Buttercup the Brave

1 It was a lovely summer day when Prince Phillip asked Aurora, "Which horse would you like to ride today?" Aurora looked around the royal stable—there were so many horses! It was hard to choose, but then she said, "From now on, I think I'd like to ride the same horse every day, that one!" "What a wonderful idea! You can have a horse of your own, just like I have Samson!" Phillip agreed.

I LIKE THIS ONE!

"I'm sure now! That's the one I like best!" Aurora exclaimed. A fine palomino warhorse had caught her eye. He was the most beautiful creature she had ever seen!

3 Aurora liked the horse even more when she rode him. "I think I'll call him . . . Buttercup," she decided. The horse snorted happily to let her know he loved his new name!

 4 Princess Aurora rode Buttercup all around the castle grounds, and when she asked him to jump over a high stone wall, he cleared it effortlessly. What a perfect and brave horse!

 5 The next day, Aurora and Buttercup set out for the fairies' cottage because she wanted to show them her magnificent new horse. So she waved goodbye to Phillip and rode into the woods.

WHAT'S THE MATTER, BUTTERCUP?

 6 But the moment they entered the woods, Buttercup became a different horse. His steps slowed to a crawl and his eyes bulged nervously. And when some of Aurora's little woodland friends appeared, Buttercup tried to spin around and run away! She could hardly believe the change in him. "What's the matter, Buttercup?" she asked, hoping to understand.

7 Aurora rode on, but she was very concerned, and decided to ask the fairies if they could help with their magic. How could a horse who was so brave at the palace be so timid in the woods?

8 When they arrived at the fairies', Flora was the first to catch sight of Buttercup. She said to Aurora, "My dear, don't worry! I'll try to help you!" And with that, she started making magic.

9 Soon Fauna and Merryweather joined them, but spell after spell all they did was change Buttercup's color! "Pink!" "Blue!" "Green!"—the fairies argued as usual.

10 When Aurora said goodbye to the fairies, she was still worried about Buttercup, who by now had returned to his original color. So she rode through the woods, thinking about what to do for him.

74

11 Lost in thought, she wasn't prepared when suddenly a mountain lion appeared, blocking their path! To her surprise, this time Buttercup didn't panic—he rose up on his hind legs to defend her!

12 Without fear, he planted his hooves and snorted angrily at the mountain lion. The big cat didn't like that at all and let out a yowl as he raced away into the woods. What courage, Buttercup!

I LOVE SUMMER RIDES!

The End

13 Buttercup was proud of himself because he had been so brave in facing the mountain lion! How relieved he was now! When a butterfly fluttered nearby and landed right on his nose, Aurora reminded him to stay calm, but he had no more fears. He smiled at the butterfly and Aurora smiled, too. What a perfect end for a wonderful summer day!

Horseriding

Good job, Buttercup! Aurora is glad her horse overcame his fears.
Take this test to see how well you remember the story.

Which horse does Aurora choose to ride?

Who does Aurora say goodbye to before riding into the woods?

What does Buttercup stand up to in the woods?

Answers on page 172

Which clumsy fairy cast this spell on Buttercup? To find out, begin with the letter F and move clockwise, crossing out the Ps. Then write the letters in the blanks below.

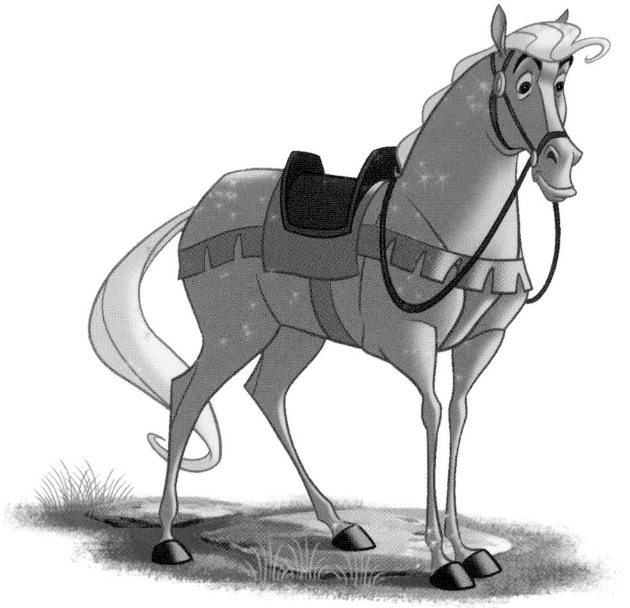

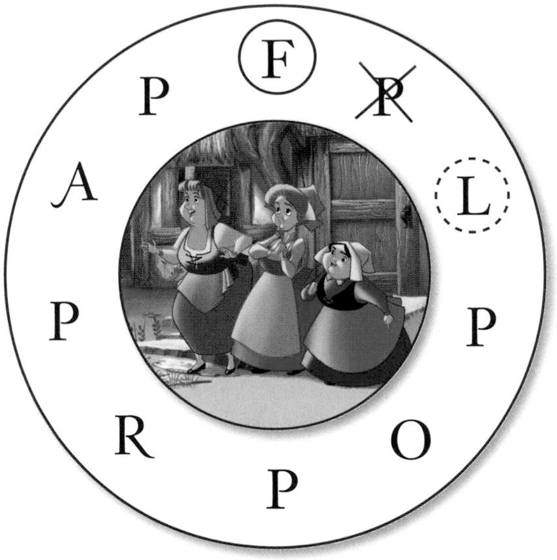

F _ _ _ _

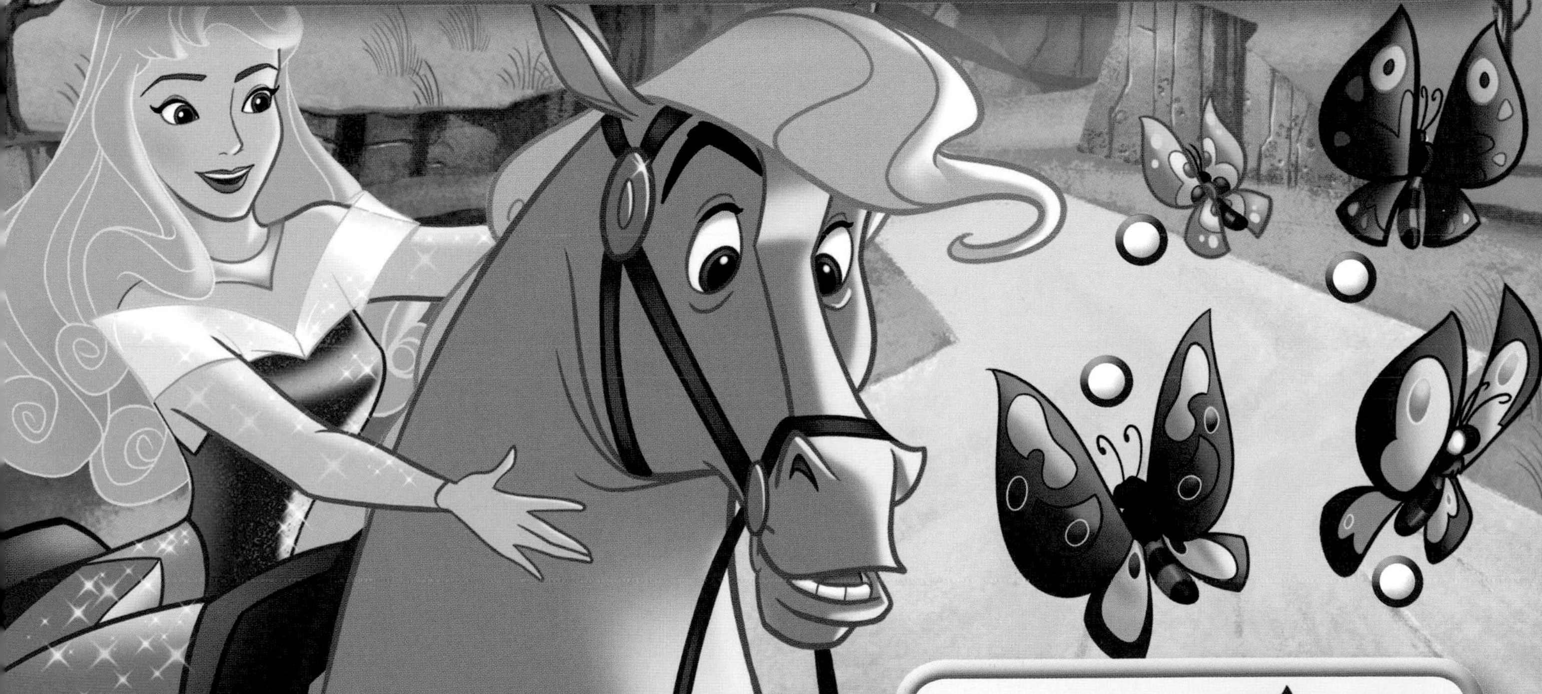

Buttercup makes friends with the butterflies. Whose shadow is shown here? Check the butterfly above.

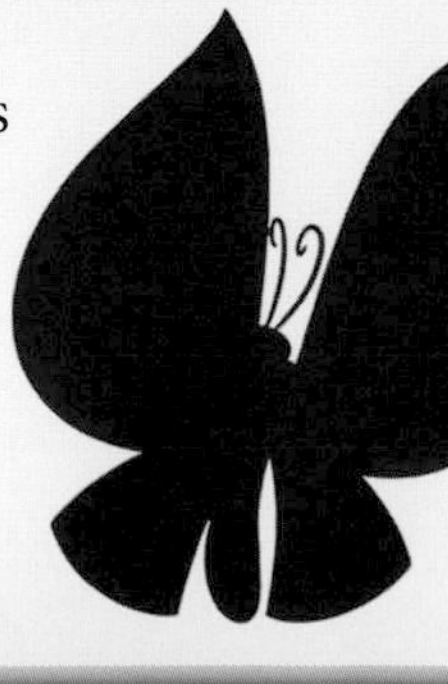

Strolling in Pixie Hollow

FLOWER GARDEN

BEACH

IN THE FLOWER GARDEN WITH . . .

ROSETTA!

You're not a big finder of Lost Things, but if you have to go looking for them, you prefer to do it surrounded by sweet-smelling flowers! Like Rosetta, you may appear distracted at times, but in reality you're always very careful and know how to make the right idea "bloom" when you need it!

ON THE BEACH WITH . . .

TINKER BELL!

You love the sound of the waves washing up against the shore and the smell of the fresh, salty sea air. You're an adventurer who loves making new discoveries, just like Tinker Bell, and you also enjoy making original and useful creations with your hands!

Which Pixie Hollow location would you like to visit in search of Lost Things? Make your choice and discover the fairy you're most like!

PINE GROVE

LILY POND

IN THE PINE GROVE WITH . . .

FAWN!

What could be more fun than looking for Lost Things with your little forest friends? Like Fawn, you adore walking over a soft carpet of pine needles and, if you're lucky, finding a lost "toy" to bring back to life!

AT THE LILY POND WITH . . .

SILVERMIST!

Like Silvermist, you enjoy peaceful places where you can take a walk with your best friend as you chat and exchange secrets. Every time you find a Lost Thing, you wonder how that object has come to you!

Blaze

Tiny and bright, he loves to fly with Tinker Bell in search of new adventures!

Blaze met Tinker Bell while she was searching for the magic Mirror of Incanta. He won the tinker fairy's heart with his cuddly cuteness and became her blazing travel companion!

Since then, this brave little firefly has been fluttering around Tinker Bell with all the enthusiasm of a lovable pup! Through thick and thin, he's always by her side, cheering her up with his charm or shining a light through even the darkest times!

Use your colored pencils to make Blaze's magic light shine!

Find 'em All!

Fawn wants to say hello to all of her pill-bug friends! Help her find them.

Start from the one behind the leaf and get to the one behind the flower. Find a path where Fawn can greet them all, and remember—no backtracking!

Answer on page 172

81

Royal Invitation

Rapunzel has put her passion for art to work and created handmade invitations for her party. Use the secret code to see the message she writes to her friends.

Answer on page 172

Being elegant for her guests is important for Rapunzel. Color her dress below to match this one.

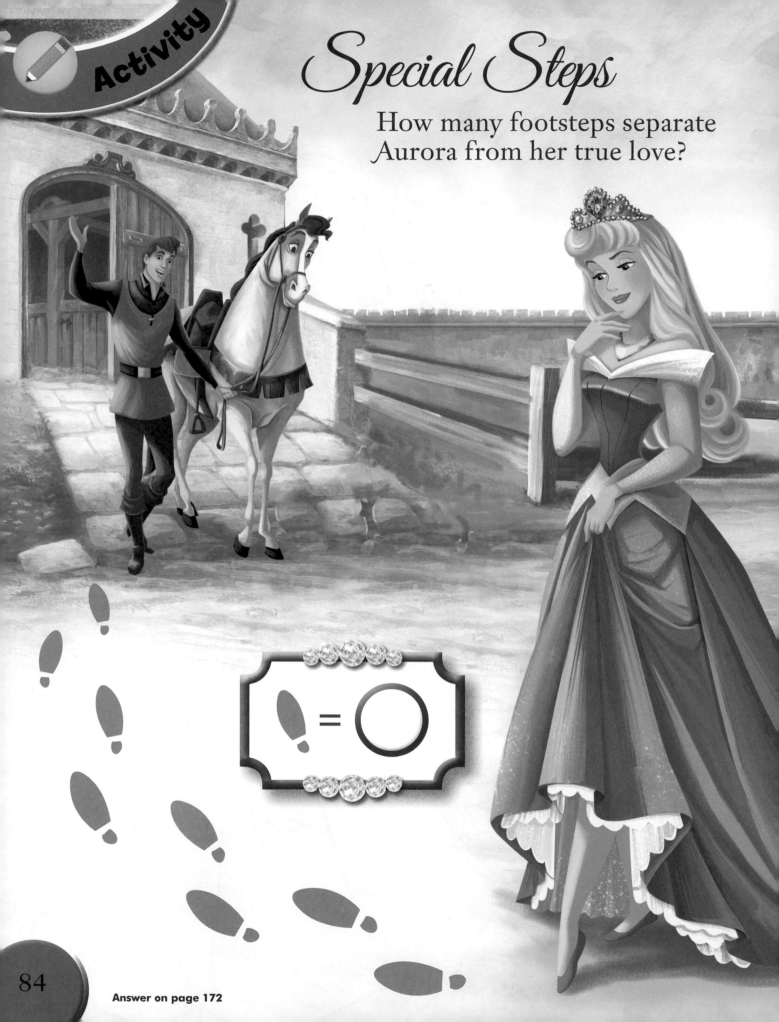

Special Steps

How many footsteps separate Aurora from her true love?

84

Answer on page 172

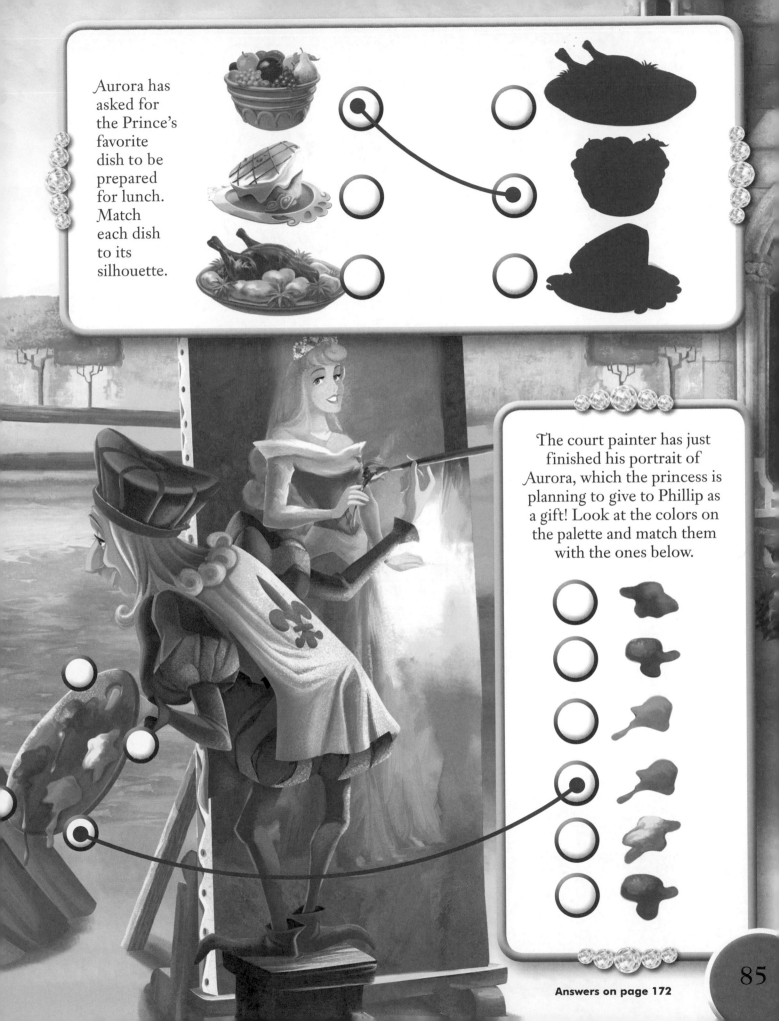

Aurora has asked for the Prince's favorite dish to be prepared for lunch. Match each dish to its silhouette.

The court painter has just finished his portrait of Aurora, which the princess is planning to give to Phillip as a gift! Look at the colors on the palette and match them with the ones below.

85

Answers on page 172

Prepare for Pet Sitting

WOULD YOU LIKE A CHANCE TO TAKE CARE OF CUTE ANIMALS AND MAKE SOME POCKET MONEY? MAYBE YOU COULD BE A PET SITTER!

What could be better than spending time with fun, cuddly pets? For animal lovers, pet sitting—feeding, caring for, and playing with an animal while the owner is away—can be the perfect first-time job.

Be Prepared!

Do some research and get all the information you can about the kind of animal you'll be caring for—favorite foods, habits, personality, and so on. Then ask the owner about specific needs of the pet you'll be sitting, like his daily routine and if he has any medical problems or favorite toys.

Quick Check

Are You a Pet Pro?

DO YOU HAVE ENOUGH PET EXPERIENCE TO BE A SITTER? THIS QUIZ WILL GIVE YOU A CLUE!

1

How much do you know about pets?

A I've read lots of articles about pet behavior
B I mostly just know about my own pet
C I think they're cute

3

How do you get along with most pets?

A They love me!
B I'm pretty comfortable with them
C Some of them make me nervous

5

How do you handle an emergency?

A I'm calm and capable
B I get anxious, but I can follow instructions about what to do
C I'm pretty freaked out!

2

How much responsibility have you had with a pet?

A Feeding, walking, training—I do it all!
B I feed my own pet
C I've never cared for an animal by myself

4

Why is it important to get to know a pet before sitting with him?

A Because it might lessen the stress of his owners being gone
B So you can find out if you like the pet
C I have no idea

Mostly **A**s:

PET PRO

You just might have **the skills necessary to become** a pet sitter!

Mostly **B**s:

IN TRAINING

You're on your way, but **you need more experience—** and start with just one pet at a time!

Mostly **C**s:

ROOKIE

If you want to pet sit, **start with something easy to care for**, like a turtle or a goldfish.

Sign Up!

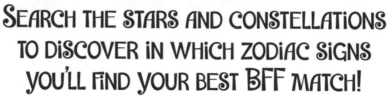

SEARCH THE STARS AND CONSTELLATIONS TO DISCOVER IN WHICH ZODIAC SIGNS YOU'LL FIND YOUR BEST BFF MATCH!

Ancient Greek philosophers identified **Fire, Earth, Air,** and **Water** as elements of the universe. The idea was that these elements rule areas of the universe, and each possesses different individual characteristics. Each of the **12 signs of the zodiac** is associated with one of these elements.

★ It's Elemental

In astrology, every zodiac sign is associated with certain characteristics that reflect its element. Fire and Air signs are considered extroverted, and Water and Earth signs are introverted.

Fire signs are bright and strong. They like to take charge. **Earth signs** are solid, like a rock—and changing their mind is like moving a mountain! The communicators of the zodiac, social **Air signs** are always on the move. Like flowing liquid, **Water signs** are adaptable and conform to the world around them.

It's interesting to learn about your element and compare your characteristics to your sign. But what about your ideal BFF? If you find your friend isn't your exact elemental match, don't worry—**what matters is that you have fun and stick together**!

Who's Your Best BFF?

CHECK A TOTAL OF SEVEN WORDS FROM ALL THE LISTS BELOW THAT BEST DESCRIBE YOUR IDEAL BFF. THEN FIGURE OUT YOUR RESULT!

- **A** Active
- **A** Leader
- **A** Self-confident
- **A** Dramatic
- **A** Spontaneous
- **A** Adventurous

- **B** Solid
- **B** Constructive
- **B** Sensible
- **B** Practical
- **B** Tidy
- **B** Patient

- **C** Curious
- **C** Imaginative
- **C** Clever
- **C** Flexible
- **C** Sociable
- **C** Observant

- **D** Instinctive
- **D** Sensitive
- **D** Protective
- **D** Creative
- **D** Mysterious
- **D** Sentimental

Mostly **A**s:

FIRE SIGN
Aries (March 21–April 19), Leo (July 23–August 22), Sagittarius (November 22–December 21).
Your ideal BFF is a powerhouse—confident, charismatic, and a blast to be around!

Mostly **B**s:

EARTH SIGN
Taurus (April 20–May 20), Virgo (August 23–September 22), Capricorn (December 22–January 19).
You'd like a BFF who can keep you grounded and support you with good advice.

Mostly **C**s:

AIR SIGN
Gemini (May 21–June 20), Libra (September 23–October 22), Aquarius (January 20–February 18).
Your best bet for a BFF is someone who's smart, sociable, and interested in lots of different things!

Mostly **D**s:

WATER SIGN
Cancer (June 21–July 22), Scorpio (October 23–November 21), Pisces (February 19–March 20).
You want a passionate, creative BFF who'll always brighten your day.

Animal Games!

Color this scene and help Fawn teach the baby bird to fly!

Join the fairies and their friends and have a great time helping them solve these puzzles!

Spot the difference!

Can you spot four differences between the two pictures of Tink's firefly friend, Blaze, below?

The Right Tails!

There's a big mix-up here! These four animals have the wrong tails. Help Fawn fix the situation. Match the animals (the numbers) to the correct tails (the letters).

1   2   3   4

a   b   c   d

The correct match-ups are: _____

Activity

A-Hunting We Will Go!

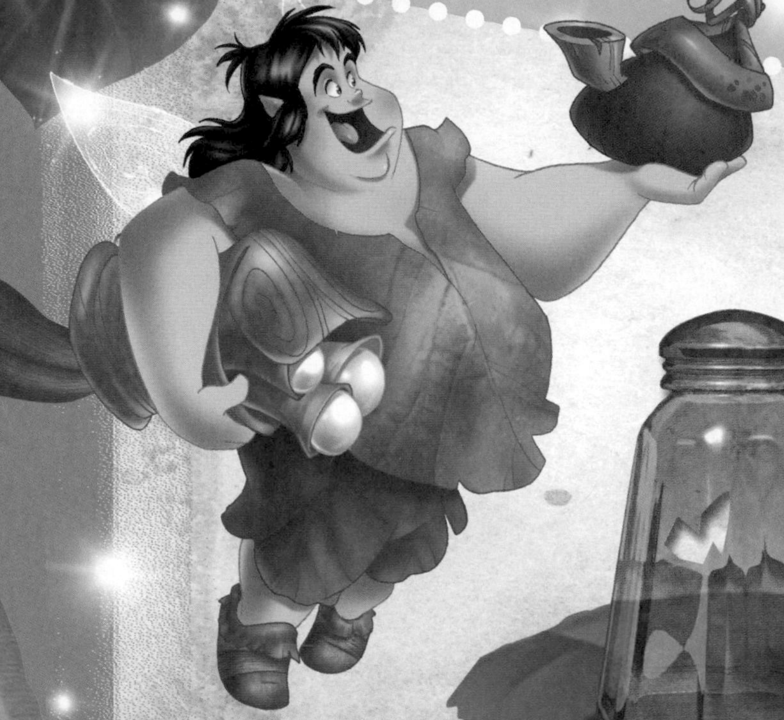

The Missing Piece

Find the right missing piece to fix the pepper shaker!

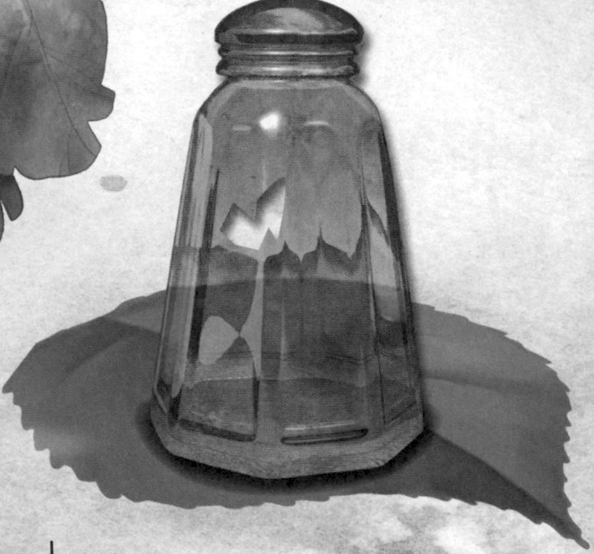

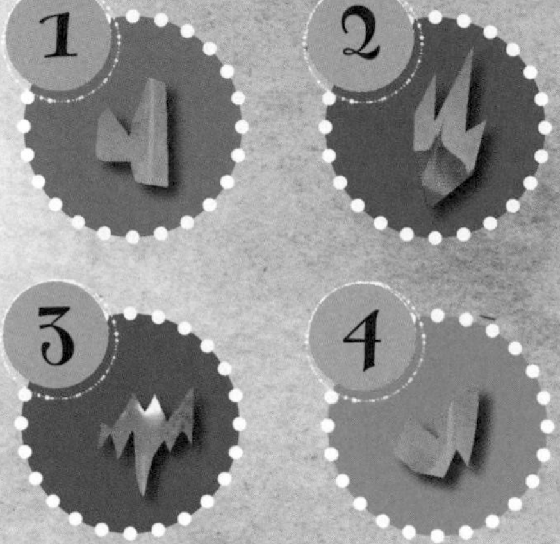
1
2
3
4

The Right Shadow

Draw lines to match each Lost Thing with its correct shadow.

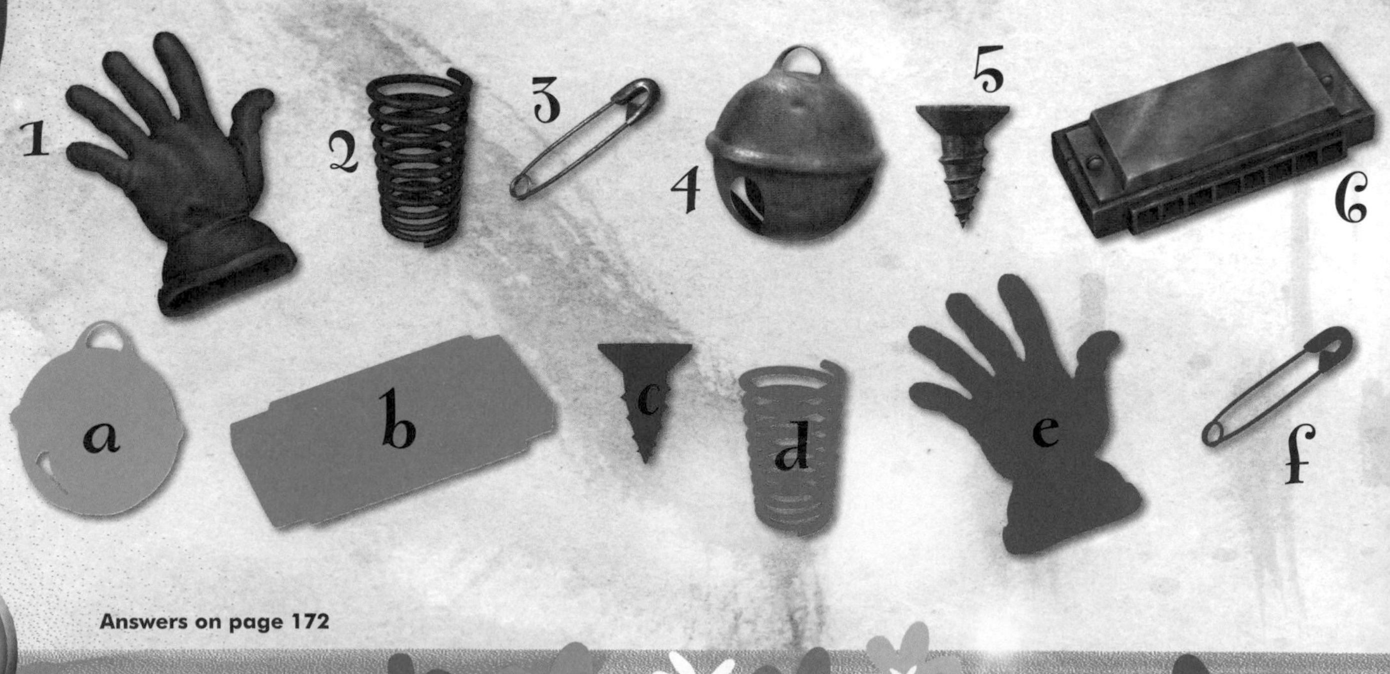
1
2
3
4
5
6
a
b
c
d
e
f

Answers on page 172

Fly with the fairies and sparrow men of Pixie Hollow in search of Lost Things!

Tinker Bell has found a very curious thing. Color this scene!

Dinnertime!

Merida has offered to help set the table for her guests, but in the confusion she's forgotten a few of them. Complete the table by putting the place settings below where they belong.

The triplets can't wait to munch on their favorite treats. Follow the paths to see which triplet eats them all!

Answers on page 172

Breakfast Time

Princess Jasmine surprises Aladdin with a delicious breakfast. Spot the five differences in these two scenes to see what she's prepared!

Jasmine has also thought about Abu and has brought him his favorite food. Do you know which one it is? Look at what he is eating and find it below.

Answers on page 172

Party Game!

To distract her guests from the idea of marrying her, Merida challenges them to a game of tic-tac-toe. It's great fun, and it turns out that McGuffin and Macintosh are no slouches. Now it's your turn!

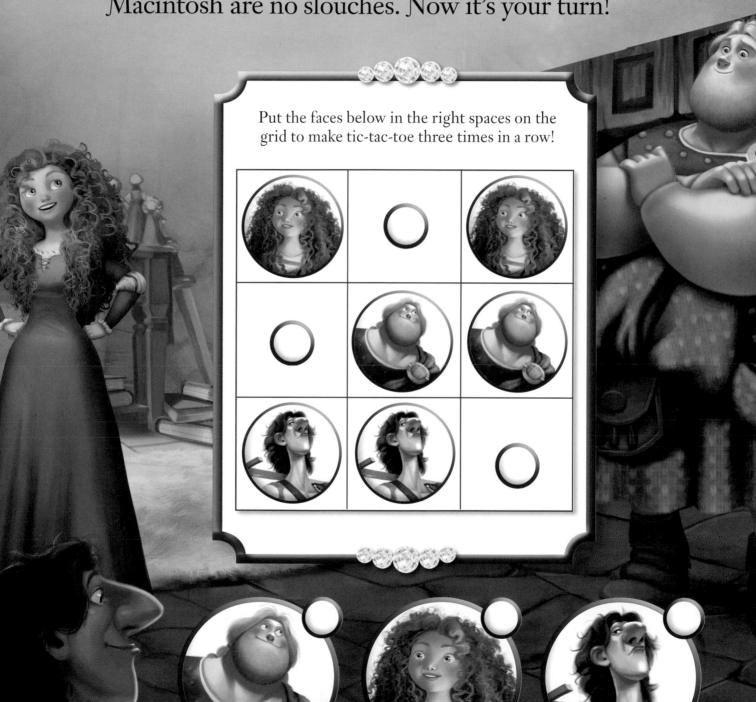

Put the faces below in the right spaces on the grid to make tic-tac-toe three times in a row!

Online Tutorial

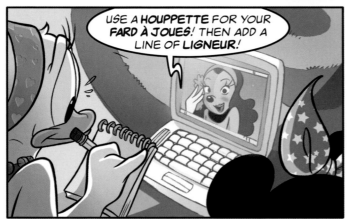

The End

Eye Magic

LEARN HOW TO USE MAKEUP TO MAKE YOUR EYES STAND OUT FOR A SPECIAL OCCASION!

Some say the eyes are the **windows to the soul**. On special occasions like parties, you could add a little "window dressing!"

To make your eyes stand out, first apply **a light shade of shadow** on the lid.

For more drama, blend **a darker shade** on the outer corner of the eye in a horizontal "v" shape.

Then add **a coat of mascara** to the lashes—colored mascara can highlight the eye color.

If you want a real party look, **paint designs on the outer corners of the eyes.**

You can even add **glitter** or **sparkles!**

Your Turn!

Practice Your Eye Look

Use crayons to practice makeup application and eye designs.

99

Get Colorful!

NOW THAT YOU KNOW HOW TO APPLY YOUR EYESHADOW, LEARN HOW TO CHOOSE THE SHADES THAT HIGHLIGHT YOUR EYE COLOR!

There are so many beautiful shades of eye shadow, how can you choose what to wear? **Your best shades depend on your skin tone and eye color.**

Color Rules

Before you shop for shadow, keep a few guidelines in mind. Bright, shimmery colors can look clownish in daylight. **Choose simple, natural shades for** everyday wear, **and save the bold colors and glitter for special occasions.**

One of the most common makeup mistakes is attempting to match eye shadow to your eye color. Instead, look for shades that softly contrast with your eyes—that's what makes eyes stand out! Colors containing red contrast with green, blue contrasts with brown.

Do It Now!

You'll Need:

Eye Shadow

Mascara

Applicator or Brush

1

Blue Eyes:
Warm shades contrast with the coolness of blue, so **soft browns**, rich **bronzes**, and **tans** make blue eyes pop—as do taupe, slate, and other natural colors. For a touch more color, try rose.

2

Green Eyes:
Purple shades are a great contrast for green eyes, so try **lavender** or **violet**. Warm mocha shades that have cool purple-ish undertones look more natural. Add more zing with pinks or apricots.

Shine Time

A little shimmer can really highlight the flecks of color in your eyes.
If the shine in your eye shadow isn't enough, add a little glitter around your eyes. Or if you're feeling especially sparkly for a party, a few shining stars will make heads turn!

Minnie's Top Tip

Shadow can irritate eyes—and make a mess if it falls on your cheeks. Before applying, tap the extra powder from your applicator.

3

Brown Eyes: You can wear almost any eye shadow color, but **greens** and **soft pinks** make your eyes stand out. Also, copper and **gold tones** highlight the typical colored flecks in brown eyes.

Mystery Tears

A NEW DAY HAS JUST BEGUN IN PIXIE HOLLOW, WHEN . . .

HI, GIRLS!

HI, TINK!

CAN YOU KEEP AN EYE ON THIS? I LEFT SOMETHING BACK AT THE HOUSE.

TSK, SAME OL' TINK!

SAME OL' VIDIA!

LEAVE IT HERE, TINK!

THANKS!

BUT WHATEVER YOU DO, DON'T OPEN IT!

OK!

WHILE THE FAIRIES AREN'T LOOKING, CHEESE APPROACHES THE MYSTERIOUS BUNDLE . . .

SNIFF SNIFF!

BUT . . .

YUCK!

SOON ENOUGH . . .

CHEESE, WHY ARE YOU CRYING?

HEY, WHAT'S THAT AWFUL SMELL BURNING MY NOSE?

SNIFF!

I CAN'T HOLD BACK THE TEARS!

WHAT . . .

OH! I FEEL LIKE... SNIFF ... CRYING!

ARE YOU ALL CRAZY?!? STOP IT RIGHT ...

SNIFF SNIFF!

... OH?!

IT MUST BE A **CRYINGITIS** EPIDEMIC!

THERE IS NO SUCH THING!

UMPF!

JUST THEN ...

GIRLS, WHAT'S GOING ON?

WE CAN'T STOP CRYING ...

AND WE DON'T KNOW WHY!

HMM... MAYBE I DO!

I **TOLD** YOU NOT TO OPEN MY BUNDLE!

WHAT'S INSIDE?!?

AN **ONION PEELER**, MY LATEST INVENTION!

GLAB!

YOU MEAN IT WASN'T CRYINGITIS!

I FORGOT THIS **MASK**! IT PROTECTS YOU FROM THE SMELL AND KEEPS YOU FROM CRYING.

ISN'T IT AN **INGENIOUS** INVENTION?

SURE, BUT TAKE IT AWAY **NOW**!

HEE! HEE!

THE END

Smell With Caution!

Just as in Pixie Hollow, there are herbs and plants on the mainland that give off such strong odors that you might have to hold your nose!

A Real Tearjerker!

Tinker Bell's onion peeler is a neat invention, but it doesn't stop the tears from flowing! When this vegetable is sliced, it releases a kind of "tear gas" that irritates the eyes.

The part of the onion we eat is the bulb, from which grows a long stem with a ball of tiny white, yellow, or pink flowers on top.

Write the name of animals that, just like stink bugs, make you hold your nose!

_____

_____

_____

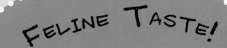

FELINE TASTE!

There are also plants with medicinal properties whose odors may be rather unpleasant, such as valerian.

Curiously, cats love valerian. All it takes are a few leaves to really cheer them up! That's why a common nickname for valerian is catnip!

SPICY PLANTS!

Some aromatic plants have very strong, pungent smells, like the fruits on a pepper tree or cloves, which are the dried flower buds of a tropical evergreen plant.

If you rub the leaves of a coriander plant, an aromatic herb similar to parsley, they give off a smell that's similar to the one released by stink bugs when they're frightened!

A Sparkling Bath!

YOU'LL NEED:

- ★ I SMALL GLASS BOTTLE WITH A CORK
- ★ SCENTED BUBBLE BATH
- ★ I CUPFUL OF COSMETIC GLITTER
- ★ I HEART—SHAPED BUTTON
- ★ I BURGUNDY EMBROIDERY THREAD OR THIN STRING
- ★ HOLE PUNCHER
- ★ PAINTBRUSH
- ★ SAFETY SCISSORS

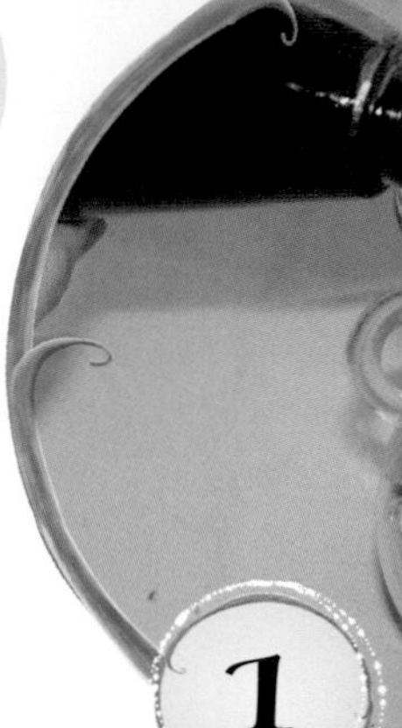

1

Pour half the glitter into the bottle, then add the bubble bath. Mix well with a paintbrush, until the glitter is evenly distributed.

TAG

✕

My fairy bubble bath

For a sweet-scented good morning, there's nothing better than an aromatic bubble bath . . . shimmering with gold! Here's a truly sparkling gift idea, for yourself or a special friend!

2

Add the remaining glitter, without mixing this time. Part of the glitter will be left on the surface to give a sparkling touch to your bubble bath.

My fairy bubble bath

3

Create your own tag like the one shown (make a hole where the X is). Thread the string through the hole and a button, then tie it to the neck of the bottle.

My fairy bubble bath

Now it's time for a bubble bath that's glittering with magic!

Incoming Ship

Ariel is waiting for her guests coming by ship. She has forgotten something! Play the game in the box below.

Ariel is not wearing shoes. Which ones do you think are right for her outfit? Check them!

Ariel has prepared a bag with special gifts for her guests.
Check off only the precious sparkling objects.

Getting Ready

Snow White is about to arrive, and the dwarves are busy trying to get the house clean and tidy. Check the characters you can see in the scene from those below.

Only one of the dwarves has not helped the others clean up. Find out his name by deleting the letter As and writing the others in the spaces.

G ~~A~~ R A U A M A P A Y

G _ _ _ _ _ _

Answer on page 173

In the Basket

Activity

Merida is preparing a basket for a delicious snack outdoors, but Harris, Hubert, and Hamish have put some strange things on the table. Draw lines to connect the right supplies to the basket, then color in the basket.

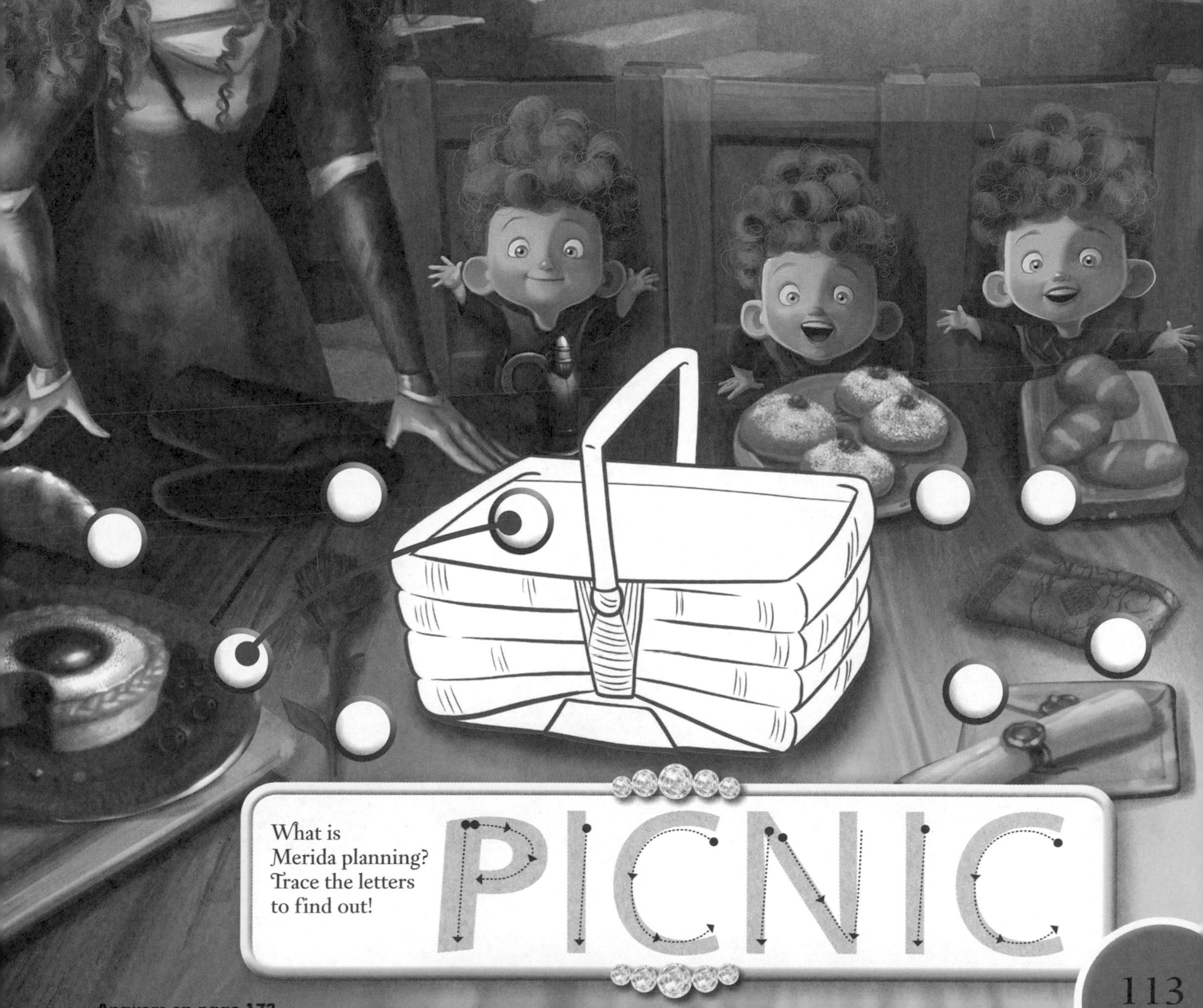

What is Merida planning? Trace the letters to find out!

PICNIC

Answers on page 173

Shake and Sparkle!

With a few simple items, it's easy and fun to make a beautiful glitter globe!

Everyone loves to play with a snow globe —just shake it up and watch snow falling magically all around a tiny scene. You can make your own, using any kind of figurine you like and adding glitter instead of snow! Just follow these easy steps!

You'll Need:

Jar

Glitter

Waterproof Glue

Figurine

Baby Oil

Make Your Own Globe

1 Remove the lid from the jar. Put a dab of glue in the center of the inside of the lid.

2 Place the figurine on the glue. Press lightly for a few seconds.

3 While the glue on the figurine dries on the lid, cover the bottom of the jar with glitter.

4 Fill the jar with baby oil, leaving a bit of room at the top.

5 Carefully tighten the lid on the jar and turn the jar over.

Now that your sparkle globe is finished, shake it and watch the glitter dance all around the figurine!

6

Use your globe as . . .

✓ a present for your bff

✓ a decorative item on your shelf

✓ a paperweight on your desk

✓ the first of a glitter globe collection

Double Up!

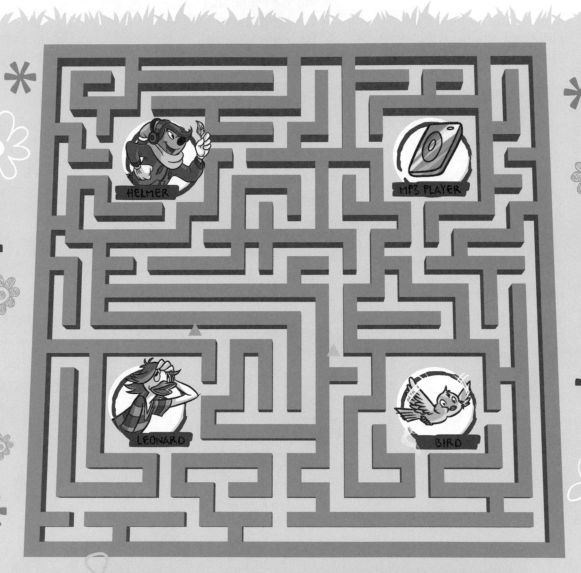

HELMER

MP3 PLAYER

LEONARD

BIRD

Dual Search!

Find the right paths through the maze to help Leonard find his
lost mp3 player and help Helmer reach the injured bird!

Answer on page 173

Pet Emergency!

If your furry friend gets hurt, do you know what to do?

Just like people, animals sometimes get sick or hurt and need **special care**. Every pet owner should know basic first-aid steps for **emergency situations!**

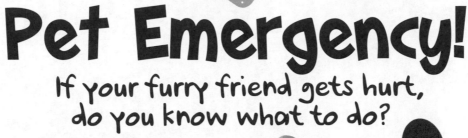

BE PREPARED!

BASIC EMERGENCY PROCEDURES:

- Always have **phone numbers** for **veterinarians** and **pet emergency clinics** handy. In an emergency, get your pet to the veterinarian **as soon as possible.**

- An animal that's hurt or frightened may **bite** or **scratch**. Be cautious, move slowly and handle with **protective gloves** if possible.

- Stop any bleeding first by applying **pressure** to the wound **with a towel or bandage.** If you must move a sick or injured animal, **wrap them in a blanket** and keep their body as stable as possible.

Tip

After treatment, your pet will need comforting, so stroke them and try to make them feel comfy and relaxed. The best medicine for your pet is your love!

FIRST-AID KIT: KEEP THESE HANDY!

GAUZE AND TAPE (FOR BANDAGING)

CLEAN TOWELS

HEAVY GLOVES

BLANKET

The Heart of Pixie Hollow

A MAGIC START

With the start of each new day, there's plenty of hustle and bustle around the Pixie Dust Tree. From beneath it rises up the Depot, where Pixie Dust is selected, checked, and dosed out under the watchful eyes of Fairy Gary.

It's here that the fairies receive their daily dose before flying off to their jobs. Tinker Bell helped build the Depot, contributing all sorts of Lost Things to make it a mechanical marvel.

There's a place in Pixie Hollow where the fairies love to fly to in the early morning: the Pixie Dust Tree!

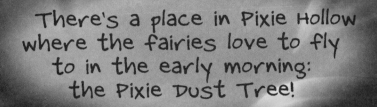

A SHIMMERING SPRING!

The beating heart of Pixie Hollow, the lush Pixie Dust Tree, is so tall it can be seen from just about anywhere in Never Land. There's a sparkling well at the top, from which Pixie Dust springs forth. It's the life-giving sap that runs up from the roots and spreads magic throughout the island!

Above the well is the Arrival Area, where new fairies flap their wings for the first time and discover their talent.

Queen Clarion lives in a chamber inside the Pixie Dust Tree, and so do the... cross out every other letter to see who else lives in the Pixie Dust Tree!

M D I O N F I P S O T K E J R C S
M O N F K T E H Y E X S O E E A P
S T O R N S S

M_____ ___ ___

_____

Answer on page 173

Tinker Bell rides Cheese as she tries to capture the sprinting thistles. Color this scene!

Little Princess

Emma has a dream that, thanks to Cinderella's help, comes true. Look at the first enchanting scene, then reconstruct the jumbled one on the right to match it!

The mice have made a real princess dress for Emma. Color in the accessories to match it.

122

One dreamy afternoon, Cinderella invited Emma to have tea with her at the castle.
Look at the scene below and check what she found on the table!

What's Cooking?

Say hello to a popular profession: It seems everyone wants to be a chef!

A chef is a professional cook who prepares and cooks food in restaurants, hotels, cafés, and other businesses. If you love to come up with your own dishes, you might one day be a famous chef!

Do You Have What It Takes?

QUICK CHECK

HERE ARE SOME TRAITS A GOOD CHEF MIGHT HAVE. CHECK OFF THE ONES THAT APPLY TO YOU!

- Food preparation skills
- Ability to handle stress
- Willingness to try new tastes
- Leadership and teamwork skills
- Cleanliness
- Creativity
- Knowledge of nutrition
- Communication skills
- Flexibility
- Organization skills

What Kind of Cook Are You?

THIS QUIZ WILL SHOW YOU!

1

Have you ever created your own recipe?

- **A** Yes, and it was delicious!
- **B** No, but I've added a twist to an existing recipe
- **C** What's a recipe?

2

When you're hungry after school, you like

- **A** A colorful plate full of interesting snacks
- **B** Heating up leftovers
- **C** Anything right out of a bag

3

At your favorite restaurant you order

- **A** Something unusual and different every time
- **B** That one special dish you can't get at home
- **C** The same thing you order at every restaurant

4

You like to spend time in the kitchen

A Trying different combinations of foods
B Making your favorite dish
C Looking in the refrigerator

Mostly **A**s:

EXPERIMENTER

Your creativity brings out your inner chef—you love to come up with your own culinary creations!

Mostly **B**s:

TECHNICIAN

You can follow a recipe flawlessly, serving up a delicious meal every time.

Mostly **C**s:

CAN OPENER

When it comes to food, you much prefer eating it to preparing it!

Star Chef

Find the perfect meals for you with this food horoscope!

ARIES
Easy-to-please Aries is up for just about anything. Try pairing a simple roasted chicken with something spicy and unexpected!

03/21–04/19

TAURUS
Taureans really know their way around a kitchen. You want your meal perfect in every detail, from the ice in the water to the flowers on the table.

04/20–05/20

GEMINI
For Geminis, variety is the spice of life. You're open to trying anything—so bring on a dish you've never tried before.

05/21–06/20

LIBRA
Libras love beautiful things, so food has to look as good as it tastes. You like to dress up your plate with garnishes and colorful dishes.

09/23–10/22

SCORPIO
Skeptical of trendy tastes, Scorpios like simple foods with basic ingredients, like steaks and salads.

10/23–11/21

SAGITTARIUS
Travel-happy Sagittarians are open to eclectic flavors. You love to try exotic dishes from all over the world!

11/22–12/21

CANCER

Family-oriented Cancers love home-cooked meals. Dig into a stew, noodles—any recipe handed down by your grandparents!

06/21–07/22

LEO

Lions are all about drama and attention. You like dressy parties with five-star gourmet foods, so you can feel like a celebrity!

07/23–08/22

VIRGO

Earthy Virgos naturally have a taste for light, organic dishes. You like to nibble on finger foods like raw veggies, cheeses, or melon balls.

08/23–09/22

CAPRICORN

Traditional Capricorns like classic, simply prepared foods. Dishes made with root vegetables like potatoes are perfect for this Earth sign.

12/22–01/19

AQUARIUS

Aquarians like food that comes from nature and are often vegetarians. Creamy soups and veggie dishes make you happy.

01/20–02/18

PISCES

Pisces are visual people—they like fancy dishes with generous portions. How about a big chocolate almond mousse?

02/19–03/20

127

An Imperfect Likeness

Let your talent shine and help the fairies solve these mysteries in a wing beat!

Here's a portrait of Terence. The artist, however, made some mistakes. Find and circle the eight details that are different from the original Terence.

Answers on page 173

A Great Passion!

Fairy Gary, head of the Pixie Dust Depot, has the biggest collection of.... Connect the dots to find out!

14 15 16 17
13 22 21 20 19 18
23   1

12   2
                      3
11   4
                5
                6
              8 7
10   9

Answer on page 173

The Pixie Dust Tree is the heart of Pixie Hollow. Use your brightest colors to make it sparkle!

Tiana and Her Unusual Guest

It was a balmy afternoon in New Orleans, and Big Daddy was in the mood for a good meal.

"Charlotte, honey!" he called out to his daughter. "How about going to Tiana's Palace for supper tonight?"

"Wonderful!" she said.

Later, as they drove to the restaurant, nobody noticed Stella the hound asleep in the back of the car. . . .

But Stella didn't mind. In fact, she didn't wake up until they reached the restaurant, where she could smell Tiana's beignets. Stella sneaked out of the car and followed her nose straight to the kitchen.

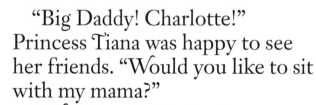

"Big Daddy! Charlotte!" Princess Tiana was happy to see her friends. "Would you like to sit with my mama?"

"Why, I can't think of anyone better to share our supper with than Eudora," Big Daddy replied.

Eudora was dining with the King and Queen of Maldonia, and little Prince Ralphie. They all greeted the new arrivals with glee: There just happened to be two free seats at their table!

131

Meanwhile, Stella smelled nothing but goodness in the kitchen.

"Lookee here!" shouted one of the cooks. "We have a visitor! Here you go, pup, have some of this gumbo. It's a new recipe! And have a juicy bone, too!"

While Stella spent a happy evening in the kitchen getting well fed and petted, Charlotte and Big Daddy dined to Louis's jazz music and enjoyed delightful conversation with their friends.

After the last song was played, the musicians put down their instruments and Louis carefully cleaned his trumpet.

For the guests, dinner was over and it was time to go. As they left, Eudora turned to Tiana and said, "Thank you! I've never heard the band play quite so well as tonight. And that new gumbo—absolutely delicious! See you later, sweetheart!"

As everyone said their goodbyes, Louis headed to the kitchen for a meal.

When Stella saw him, she was scared—she hadn't met the huge alligator before. She began to bark and growl!

Louis tried to speak to Stella. "Oh, now hold on, little dog! I'm not here to eat you. I just want a taste of the chefs' new gumbo!"

The kitchen staff backed away.

133

Princess Tiana and
Prince Naveen heard the noise
and went to the kitchen. They saw
a very frightened Stella barking at Louis!
"What's going on in here?" Tiana asked.

Tiana hugged Stella.
"Oh," she said. "It's just Louis.
He wouldn't hurt anybody."
"That's true!" Naveen
cried. "Louis? He is
nothing but a big guy
with an even bigger heart."

"Go ahead, Stella," Tiana told Stella. "Make friends with Louis!"

Stella sniffed Louis cautiously, then turned back to the food.

Naveen giggled, and Louis wanted to giggle too, but he thought he might scare Stella all over again.

When the guests had all left, the staff of Tiana's Palace put together a supper made up of that evening's leftovers. Prince Naveen played the ukulele, and Tiana baked some of her special beignets—just for Stella.

Before dawn, the prince and princess dropped Stella back at home. No one had even noticed she was missing yet!

"Good night, Stella!"

The dog gave one last woof and trotted toward the house. This had been the best night of her life!

The End

135

At Tiana's Palace

Everyone is welcome at Tiana's restaurant, where the princess treats all her clients with kindness and loving care— including Stella the dog! Take your place at Tiana's and enjoy the games on these pages.

There's a delicious smell coming from Tiana's kitchen! Help Stella follow her nose and find the way to the beignets.

Answer on page 173

The kitchen staff have treated Stella to some tasty bones, which she is gobbling up with delight. Number the bowls as they go from full to empty.

THE SEQUENCE

When they go to Tiana's Palace, customers always glue a photo of themselves inside the guest album. Find this sequence vertically, horizontally, and diagonally—it appears four times.

Answers on page 173

137

Volleybug

OUR FRIENDS IN PIXIE HOLLOW ARE PLAYING A FUN NEW GAME.

IT'S CALLED **VOLLEYBUG**. EACH TEAM POSITIONS ITSELF ON EITHER SIDE OF THE SPIDER WEBNET . . .

WHAT DO YOU PLAY IT WITH?

A BALL! THAT'S WHERE OUR FRIENDS THE PILL BUGS COME IN . . .

WHO WANTS TO GO FIRST?

IT'S A NEW GAME FOR THE PILL BUGS TOO, AND THEY'RE AFRAID . . .

NO ONE? COME ON, IT'S FUN!

A BRAVE BUG STEPS FORWARD!

READY, LITTLE BUDDY?

THE GAME BEGINS!

SWISSSSSH

HERE WE GO!

SOMEONE ALREADY APPEARS TO BE HAVING FUN . . .

YEAHHH!

MINE! MINE!

OOOOHHH

HA! HA! A DEW DROP FOR YOU . . .

WOOSH

OOOOHHH

140

Like a Ball!

Pill bugs roll themselves up into balls
when something frightens them . . .
or when your friends the fairies
want to play a game of volleybug!

SHRIMPS' LI'L COUSINS

Shy pill bugs are tiny crustaceans and the country
cousins of shrimps and crabs! They've adapted to living
out of water, but they do require damp, dark places.
You'll find them beneath pots of flowers and stones,
and sometimes in your basement.

They dine on leaves and fruits that fall
to the ground, or even organic waste they
find in the soil, and thus do their
part to create fertile terrain!

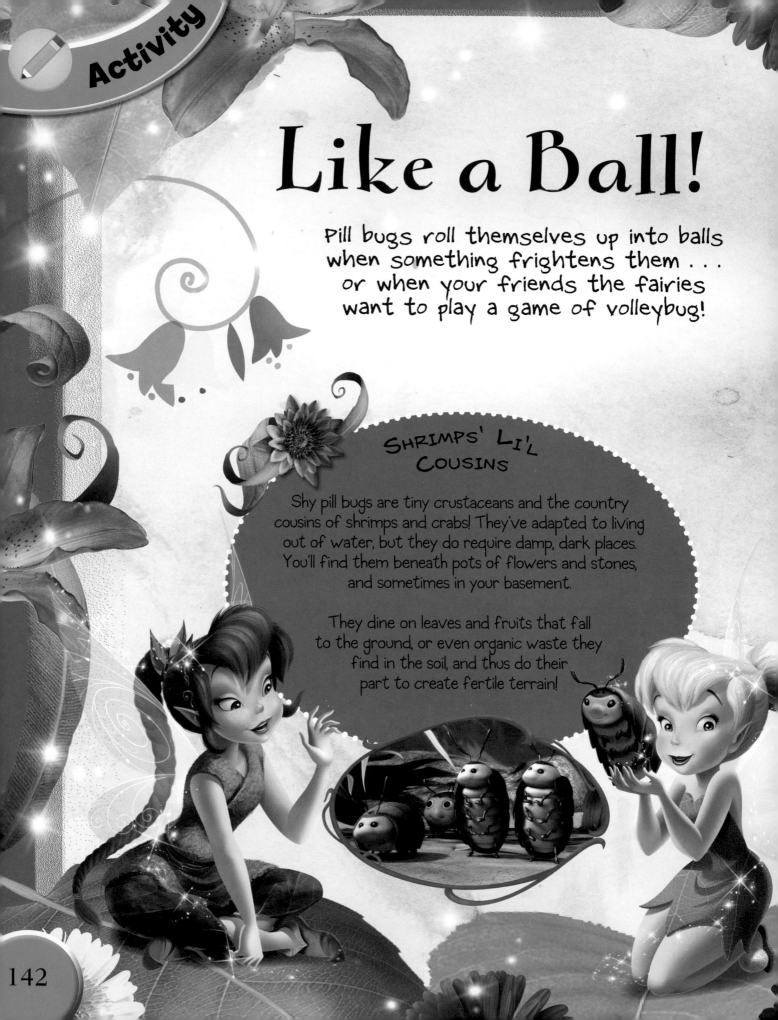

DOUBLE PROTECTION

These little creatures "wear" a sort of armor on their backs, while the front of their bodies is exposed. As soon as they feel threatened, they roll up into a ball to protect themselves.

And thanks to their coloring that blends in with the ground, they also manage to become almost invisible!

Help this pill bug return to his home under the flower pot!

1 4
2 3

Answer on page 173

Flowery Garden

Before the outdoor celebration begins, Aurora gathers flowers to offer to her guests. Cut out the pieces on the next page and assemble them to recreate this scene.

The roses are blooming in Aurora's castle! Number the bushes from the one with the least flowers to the one with the most.

○   ①   ○   ○

ASK AN ADULT FOR HELP!

 Look at the bird to the left, then check off the one that's identical.

  ○   ○  ○

145

Answers on page 173

Spring Blooms

Cinderella is filling vases with pretty flowers
to brighten up the rooms in the palace.
Help her by adding some color.

We win!

Good Sport

How much of a team player are you? Take a swing at this quiz and find out!

Do you work for the good of your team? Do you work best when you have your teammates beside you? Or do you like to set your own goals? Check off one circle for each check. Then find your level on the cooperation meter below.

1 I'm willing to compromise what I want for the good of the team.

2 I think team goals are just as important as my individual goals.

Great play, great friends!

3 I think my teammates' skills are just as important to our success as mine are.

4 I like to see my teammates perform well.

5 When I get compliments, I share credit with my teammates.

6 When a teammate makes a mistake, I encourage rather than criticize.

7 When something needs to be done and no one wants to do it, I volunteer.

◁ Cooperation Meter ▷

○ ○ ○ ○ ○ ○ ○ ○

0% ▮▮▮▮▮▮▮▮▮▮▮▮▮ 100%

8 When I see a teammate struggling, I'm quick to help, even when I'm busy elsewhere.

IT'S ALL ABOUT YOU   **LEARNING TO SHARE**   **TOTAL TEAM PLAYER**

On a String

Which necklace to wear? Follow these guidelines to pick the perfect one for any outfit!

Love it!

 tip 1

Let your necklace shine by not wearing earrings, and keep rings and bracelets to a minimum.

Wear a short choker necklace with open-collar shirts, square necklines or crew necks (as in most T-shirts).
1

With a solid-color top, you can wear a detailed, multicolored necklace.
3

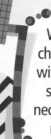 Brighten up a plain neutral color with a bright neon necklace.
2

With a boatneck top, a long, bold necklace works best.
5

 A long necklace with a pendant has a v-shape that accents a v-neck shirt.
4

 tip 2

If you're wearing a bold necklace, keep the rest of your look simple. Too many details can look too busy.

Jump for Joy!

Join the challenge and hop along with your fairy friends!

The Race Is On!

Who'll win the leapfrog tournament? Let's find out! Start at the arrow and move along the grid by following the instructions below.

Go right!   Go down!

Out of Bounds!

Before the tournament starts, a frog has hopped off....
Begin at the arrow and follow its path to see where he went.

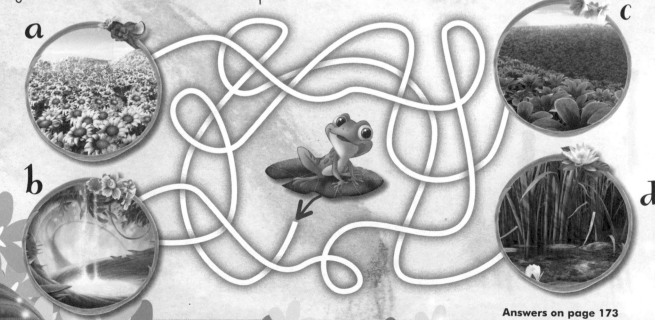

a

b

c

d

150

Answers on page 173

Silvermist needs your help to make her water games magical! Add a splash of color!

A Fresh New Look

On this beautiful spring morning, Belle is going to wear a nice dress, suited to the season. Help her choose the right accessories!

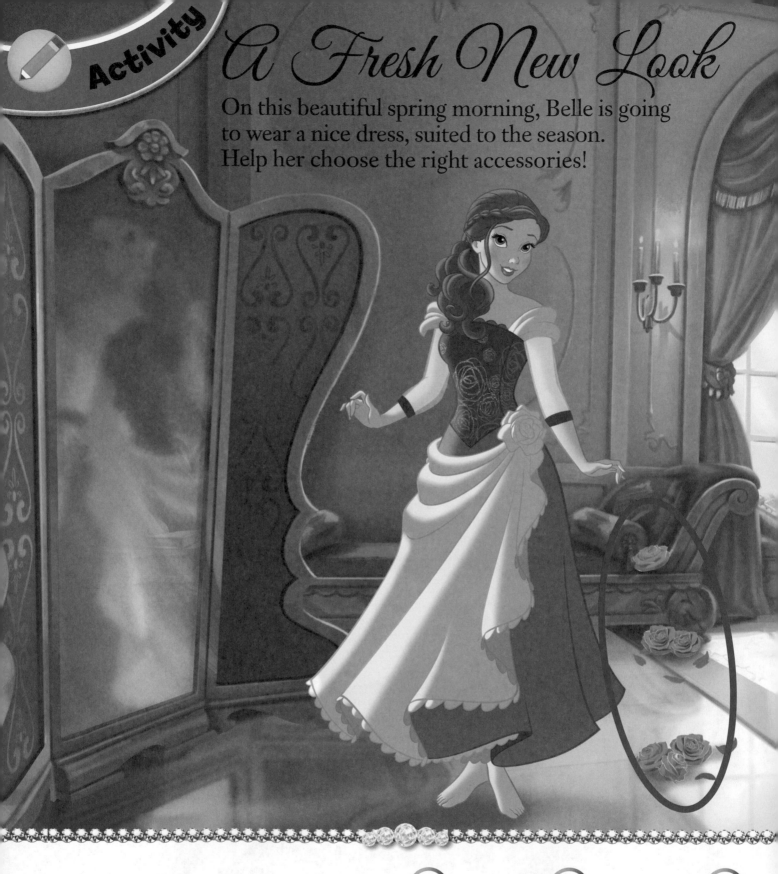

Complete Belle's fresh new outfit. Check off the springtime accessories.

What a surprise!
The Beast has
decorated Belle's room
with roses. Draw a
circle around the ones
of the same color.

153

Blossom Art

Tiana, Naveen, and Charlotte are decorating their float for the Mardi Gras Parade. Put on a few artistic touches of your own: Draw and color in the missing parts.

Charlotte wants to add a few nice details to her dress. Give her a hand with your colored pencils.

What beautiful baskets of flowers! Count them and check off the correct total.

= 2 ○   4 ○   6 ○

Which Character Are You Most Like?

This quiz will give you a clue!

1 YOUR FAVORITE ACTIVITY IS

- **A** Designing outfits
- **B** Playing sports
- **C** Daydreaming about your crush
- **D** Winning

2 FRIENDS DESCRIBE YOU AS

- **A** Cheerful
- **B** Athletic
- **C** Romantic
- **D** Ambitious

3 YOU LIKE A BFF WHO IS

- **A** Loyal
- **B** Thoughtful and sensitive
- **C** Encouraging
- **D** Willing to do what you want

4 AT SCHOOL YOU'RE KNOWN FOR YOUR

- **A** Creativity
- **B** Energy
- **C** Shyness
- **D** Competitiveness

Mostly **A**s:

MINNIE

You have a lot in common with stylish, friendly Minnie!

Mostly **B**s:

DAISY

You're always on the go, like Daisy!

Mostly **C**s:

MACY

You're most like Minnie and Daisy's colorful friend Macy!

Mostly **D**s:

ABIGAIL

You could be the queen of your school, like Abigail!

Hat Hunt

There's a hat for any occasion— you just have to find the right one!

Get a Clue

Every explorer needs the right gear to take along on his or her adventures— including the correct hat! Follow the clues below and cross out all the poor choices to find the perfect explorer hat!

1 The hat must be **sturdy,** so a pointy paper party hat will not do!

2 The hat must have a **wide** brim **all the way around** to protect the explorer from sun and rain.

3 A plain, **earthy color** with **no flashy details** is best, so that the hat blends with the natural environment.

157

Answer on page 173

Which Creative Career Is for You?

To discover the job that best displays your creativity, take this quiz!

Inspiration!

1

You find it easiest to remember things

Ⓐ That you hear
Ⓑ That you see
Ⓒ That you write down

2

My favorite part of a movie is

Ⓐ The soundtrack
Ⓑ The beautiful scenery
Ⓒ The clever dialogue

3

In my free time I like to

Ⓐ Play or listen to music
Ⓑ Draw or paint
Ⓒ Read or write stories

4

Which describes you?

Ⓐ I hum or sing all the time
Ⓑ I like to work with my hands
Ⓒ I get lost in my thoughts a lot

5

Your bedroom is filled with

Ⓐ CDs, musical instruments, or sheet music
Ⓑ Your own artwork
Ⓒ Books

Mostly As:

MUSICIAN

You like to express your feelings and thoughts through your musical ability.

Mostly Bs:

ARTIST

You create artwork that reflects how you look at the world.

Mostly Cs:

WRITER

Your lively imagination allows you to create fascinating stories.

Busy Pets

Don't let your pets get bored: Follow these tips to keep them happy!

Just like people, animals can get **bored and lonely.** Your pet can't tell you when they're bored, but you can see the signs. A bird might get stressed and pull out feathers. And when your dog doesn't have anything better to do, they might just chew on the sofa! **Fight boredom by keeping your pet busy and happy.** The five tips below can help!

1

EXERCISE
Let your pet **burn off energy** by walking, running, or playing daily.

PLAY TIME
Make sure you give your pet plenty of **interesting toys.**

2

3

FURRY BUDDIES
Give them a playmate to keep them company. For a dog, you could plan a **play date** with other dogs.

4

BE A BFF
Spend time with your pet! They can't be bored when they're with their best friend!

5

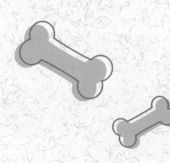

TRICKS
Training sessions keep your **pet's brain active** and prevent boredom.

A Friend by Your Side

THERE ARE TIMES WHEN THE HOURS SEEM TO DRAG ON **ENDLESSLY**!

SIGH! FALL IS SO BORING!

OH, I WISH THERE WAS SOMETHING FUN TO DO!

HMM . . . MAYBE I HAVE AN IDEA!

AND OTHER TIMES WHEN YOU LOSE TRACK OF THEM BECAUSE . . .

. . . YOU'RE HAVING SO MUCH **FUN**!

EVEN WHEN YOU NEVER THOUGHT YOU WOULD!

AND WHEN THAT HAPPENS, ONE THING'S FOR SURE . . .

THINGS ARE NEVER BORING . . .

. . . WITH A LITTLE IMAGINATION AND A **FRIEND** BY YOUR SIDE!

Manuscript: Valentina Camerini Art: Paolo Campinoti Ink: Roberta Zanotta Paint: Angela Capolupo Graphic illustrations: Giuseppe Fontana

THE END

Dream Gown!

For moonlight celebrations, the fairies wear fantastic evening gowns. Which one suits you? Take your pick!

PLAYFUL!

Like FAWN, you adore outfits that wrap you in a warm embrace, while leaving you the freedom you need to dance and play!

BUBBLY!

Your style is fresh and fizzy! Like SILVERMIST, you're full of life and upbeat, but tender and sensitive, too.

SPARKLING!

You're bright and sunshine-y, even in evening attire! And like IRIDESSA, you inspire good cheer and positive feelings!

UNIQUE!

You like being original. The perfect evening gown for you is one you've designed yourself! Like TINKER BELL, you're creative and your style is a reflection of your adventurous spirit!

A Sweet Royal Visit

1 One morning that seemed like all the rest, a carriage came to a halt before a school. "The princess is coming!" a crowd of girls cried. Cinderella was there to pay them a visit!

2 The headmistress of the school scurried to the door and opened it wide. "Welcome, Your Highness!" she said. She and the girls curtsied as Cinderella entered the room.

3 "It's so nice to see you all," said the princess. Everyone was glad to have Cinderella as their guest. No one was more excited than Emma, who simply adored her. They all spent a fun afternoon together! Then Cinderella surprised them by announcing, "In one week's time, there will be a grand ball at the castle—to be held in your honor. You'll wear the dresses I am having made for each of you, of course."

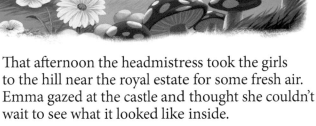

4 That afternoon the headmistress took the girls to the hill near the royal estate for some fresh air. Emma gazed at the castle and thought she couldn't wait to see what it looked like inside.

5 Soon, Emma noticed a group of seamstresses approaching the castle gates. *Hmm, maybe when they go inside I can get a peek of the courtyard,* she thought. So she ran toward the castle and hid among them.

WHAT A FANCY DRESS!

6 Emma managed to sneak in and soon found herself in a room down the hall, where the seamstresses were cutting silk, satin, and velvet. "Come in!" one of them called. She thought Cinderella had sent her to model the dresses and began draping fabric over her. When Cinderella stopped by a little while later, she cried "Oh, my! You look beautiful!" She thought Emma had come to the castle with the seamstresses, so she didn't worry.

165

I'D LOVE TO HELP YOU!

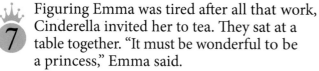

7 Figuring Emma was tired after all that work, Cinderella invited her to tea. They sat at a table together. "It must be wonderful to be a princess," Emma said.

8 Cinderella laughed. "There's much more to being a princess than clothes and parties," she replied. "Why don't you help me this afternoon and see what else a princess does?"

YOU LOOK STUNNING!

9 The princess was always very busy making sure things ran smoothly, and preparing supplies to the poor and hungry. Emma saw that being a princess wasn't as easy as she thought.

10 Cinderella and Emma put together baskets of food, clothing, books, and toys for schools and orphanages around the kingdom. Emma loved looking for old clothes in Cinderella's wardrobe.

11 When they arrived at Emma's school to deliver some baskets, the girl told everybody her adventure. Cinderella was happy to invite Emma to go to the castle every day and help her with her duties.

12 Emma started visiting Cinderella every day. She loved helping the princess, especially with party planning. How thrilling it was to see the mice sewing a dress for her!

The End

13 At last, the night of the ball arrived. The girls twirled across the dancefloor in their magnificent new dresses. "I still wish I could be a real princess," said Emma. Cinderella replied with a smile, "Because you've worked so hard, I'm going to make you an honorary princess for the evening." "Oh, thank you!" the girl cried, thrilled that she'd get to be Princess Emma for one magical night.

Draw Tinker Bell

In four simple steps we'll show you how to draw your curious, fearless, yet charming and lovable fairy friend: Tinker Bell.

Then turn the page and give it a try!

1 DRAW THE OUTLINES: A CIRCLE FOR HER HEAD, AN OVAL FOR HER TRUNK, AND A SOMEWHAT FLATTENED CIRCLE FOR HER HIPS. THEN SKETCH HER ARMS AND LEGS.

2 DRAW IN FACIAL FEATURES AND BODY DETAILS, AND THE OUTLINE OF HER DRESS AND THE POMPOMS ON HER SHOES.

YES!
bottom of skirt
pointy like leaves

NO!
bottom of skirt not
shaped like flower petals

3

Give definition
to her face and
body, and draw
her wings.
Then "clean up"
your drawing
by erasing
the outlines.

4

Now color
her in with your
brightest crayons!

169

Now that you've seen all the steps to draw Tink, try to do it yourself! Practice here—trace the gray lines with your pencil and then color her in.

Page 6
The paint sprayer

Page 14
A carrot

Page 16

horseriding

Page 21
A—2, B—2, C—3, D—2, E—4
A crow hops out of Tink's basket

Page 22
a—1, b—4, c—2, d—3

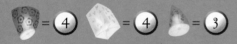

Page 24

Page 25

Pages 26 & 27

Page 30
Shadow 3

Page 31
a—2, b—3, c—1
Path B

Page 32

Page 33
a has four strings, b has three

Page 41
A shell

Page 52

Page 53
3 is the correct missing piece

Page 54
love
freedom
luck

Pages 56 & 57

Page 58
A—I, B—J, C—G, D—H, E—Q, F—S,
K—N, L—O, M—P, R—T

Earplugs A are plugged in

Page 59

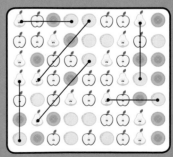

A—2, B—1, C—3, D—4

Page 61
Stridulation

Page 62
Vidia—1, Periwinkle—3, Iridessa—4,
Tinker Bell—5, Fawn—2

Page 64

A—False, B—True, C—False, D—True

Page 71
A—True, B—False, C—False,
D—False, E—True

Spill C is the perfect match

Page 76

Page 77
FLORA

172

Page 81

Page 82
COME TO MY BIRTHDAY

Page 84
8 steps

Page 85

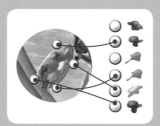

Page 91

1—d, 2—a, 3—b, 4—c

Page 92
4 is the missing piece
1—e, 2—d, 3—f, 4—a, 5—c, 6—b

Page 94

Page 95

Page 96

Page 97

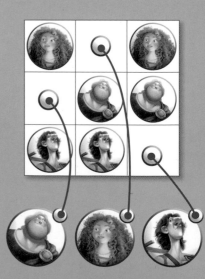

Page 110

Page 111

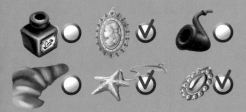

Page 112
GRUMPY

Page 113

PICNIC

Page 116

Page 119
MINISTERS OF THE SEASONS

Page 123

① ④ ⑦ ③ ⑥ ⑤ ② ⑧

Page 128

Page 129
Pixie Dust teacups

Page 136

Page 137

① ④

② ③

Page 137

Page 143
4 is the correct path

Page 145

③ ① ④ ②

Page 150

 Fawn

d—the pond

Page 152

Page 155
There are 6 baskets of flowers in total

Page 157

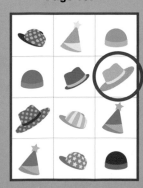